Sanitarium #016

First Published 2013 by Eye Trauma Press

This electronic edition published 2013 by Eye Trauma Press

Thank you to all of our contributors, we couldn't of done it without you.

Contents

ISSUE SIXTEEN

Dear Reader,

At this time of year it is nice to pull up a seat and drink long into the night with friends by your sides. Speaking of the year past and the mysteries that the next 12 months might bring.

New years resolutions are made, only to be broken moments after the clock strikes midnight. However I do look back over the past 12 months with fondness and cheer. I have met some great new friends and worked with some interesting characters.

We have seen some great projects being, some fall by the wayside and even some rise from the ashes to begin anew. We have also lost a few of the greats this year, but old masters have also returned with sequels that saw them rise again in the best-seller lists where they belong.

The team at Sanitarium has grown and we hope to continue this in the New Year. So here I raise my glass to you and wish you a Merry Christmas and very Happy New Year.

We hope you enjoy the stories, dark verse, interviews and the rest of the goodies in this issue.

Welcome to the Sanitarium

Barry Skelhorn
Editor

BIG BAD – AN ANTHOLOGY OF EVIL VOL 2

Send us your best short story that features a bad guy or evil character as the protagonist. It can be fantasy, urban fantasy, superhero, sci-fi, horror, whatever. Just send us your best bad guy story. We're taking ten. That's right, there are only ten slots available in this anthology.

Deadline: January 1, 2014
Length: 3,000-9,000 words
Payment: Royalties

WHAT HAS TWO HEADS, TEN EYES, & TERRIFYING TABLE MANNERS?

Mega Thump Publishing is looking for quality short stories that mix both science fiction and horror elements. Evil robots, mad scientists, bloodthirsty aliens, and haunted spaceships would all qualify. Think of films like ALIEN, THE THING, EVENT HORIZON,INVASION OF THE BODY SNATCHERS, THE BLOB, PHANTASM, and FROM BEYOND.

As long as they fit the above criteria, stories can be horrifically humorous or dead serious in tone. They can be completely over-the-top in gore, sex, and any nastiness you can think of (no YA stuff here). They can even be thought-provoking. Most importantly, all stories must be well-written and entertaining.

Deadline: January 1, 2014
Length: 1,000-15,000 words
Payment: $20 + contributor copy (print or digital)

SHADOWS & TALL TREES

I publish quiet, literary horror fiction. Fiction that is offbeat and eclectic; dark, bizarre and psychological. Stories both subtle and prosaic. Weird, strange tales. Ghost stories. Shadows & Tall Trees is a literary journal of the dark and fantastic, with mainstream sensibilities. I am seeking low-key, literary horror.

Deadline: April 1, 2014 (or until filled)
Length: Up to 7,500 words. Also accepting non-fiction up to 2,500 words.
Payment: 1 cent per word (max $50) + 2 contributor copies

DARK FUSE: ANTHOLOGY SERIES

DarkFuse is an anthology series (published up to 4 times per year) collecting the finest short stories in the modern era of dark fiction. It is published by DarkFuse, the premier dark fiction publisher, and continues the objective of the company's successful novel and novella book line, which is to produce high quality fiction from both established and undiscovered authors.

Each new volume will feature 6 original short stories, all with a dark edge.

Deadline: Ongoing
Word Count: 2K-5K
Payment: $50 on acceptance plus 5% of revenue per author from sales of the eBook anthology. Each contributor will receive a copy of the limited hardcover edition.
Fiction: Horror, thriller, suspense, crime, sci-fi, bizarre—anything with a dark slant. Original, never-before-published stories. No reprints.

BONES

There are bones of the dead everywhere, and they're sharp. Under your feet as you walk across your yard, in the cement of buildings, under the foundation of your home, in the coffee you drink, in the food you eat. Science estimates 100 billion human beings have lived and died. There are bones everywhere. There are skeletons everywhere, from universities to unnamed places we really don't want to know about. We love skeletons as we are walking skeletons. There's an old phrase about skeletons in the closet. What if the skeleton in your closet is real? Hell, maybe you own a skull and it's placed near your computer as your skeletal fingers press the keyboard. When we look at strangers, friends and family we fail to see the skull behind the face. And the eyes of skulls are dark and deep. Dig deep and give me a story about bones.

Deadline: Open until filled
Length: Flash Fiction (up to 1,000 words), Poetry (any length), Short Fiction (up to 5,000 words) there will be two Editor's Choice Awards for $25 each.

THESE VAMPIRES DON'T SPARKLE

At Sky Warrior Books, we're not above…well, anything. Hence, we love Vampires – but NOT the sparkly kind. We're betting you love vampires too. So, send us your best work on vampires, original or reprint (must have the rights). Can be fiction, nonfiction, or poetry. Sure, we'll take standard horror and dark fantasy, but you can be creative. Vampires in space, vampire critters, vampire love stories (uh, no erotica or sparkles), fantasy vampires, steampunk vampires, vampire humor (a strong plus), vampires on stakes…well, you get the idea.

Deadline: March 15, 2014
Length: 500-7,000 words
Payment: Royalties
Submission Guidelines

If you have some news to share with us at Sanitarium please send an email to:

editor@sanitariummagazine.com

We look forward to hearing from you.

CLAYTON HILL SANITARIUM

Come and Stay

Jim Markus

Physician: Dr. Roundtree
8245-AVD12

d ca
etails
that w
her fla
was a y
was that
never

8

A magic of before our time
taught and learned within a rhyme
forever remember this prayer benign
or suffer we must for another's crime

build thy blessings strong as stone
and forever may devils rest alone
until an heir reclaims the throne
then blood for blood and bone for bone

pray o angels come and stay
lest we ever go astray
keep all children safe today
never never go away

- Unknown

Eric pulled his knapsack tight against his body, stepped into the wet soil, and twisted himself around the gatepost. He followed the path through twists and turns all the way to the top of the hill. Ahead of him, the driveway circled around a fountain and up to the grand entrance. It was the single largest residence he had ever seen. Gargoyles glared down from carved turrets. Vines clung to every wall, sometimes more dense than the stones they covered. Gusts of wind pounded against the mass of stones and windows lining the wide estate. Here, hidden in the old pine forest, was a castle.

The original building plans had been published with the rest of the town records a century ago. Earlier that day, he had dusted them off in the basement of the town's library. They had shown a three-story, six-bedroom house. The building in front of him now boasted ten times as many rooms. The shipping business of the age could be lucrative, he knew, but this was excess. He counted six miniature towers. Six pillars supported the front entablature, a cracked stone piece that dominated the entryway. Guest houses, each twice the size of his own house, dotted the outer rim of the property. Many lacked walls. Most still stood, scattered bones in an untended garden.

Eric walked into the portico and ran his fingers across the sculptures carved into the doors. He brushed the wings of angels, down the long swords they held, and onto the faces of the howling demons below. Normally, even wooden sculptures looked like candle wax by the time he saw them. The sharp edges of the jagged faces pricked at his digits. If we can smooth it, he thought, we could replicate the design for key chains in the gift shop.

Leaves rustled over his shoulder. Eric turned, but nothing was there.

He walked toward the fountain, near a trio of maple trees that shaded it from the setting sun. A single stone statue stood in the center. It might make a perfect family picnic area. A heavy groan wailed from above. Eric flailed his arms and fell backwards as a branch, the size of a man, crashed down in front of him. Catching himself hard on one arm, he braced against the wind. He was shaking. His light jacket whipped back and forth as he sat. A storm of leaves and needles flew past his face. The flesh on his hands stung as he gripped his lapels tightly against his body and squinted at the house. The windows looked back at him through the torrent of blowing leaves.

That's near enough to death for today, Eric thought as he climbed to his feet. The house could wait for another day.

***

"Every one of these projects has finished sooner than I've expected." Eric crouched next to a stack of books that Laura had set aside and started sorting through them. His gray eyes scanned the bindings. "Everybody wants to see these buildings restored." He pulled an old photograph from the inside cover of the top copy, a black-and-white snapshot of a brick factory building. Three men in dark suits smiled back from the front of the building. "Do you remember this one?" He asked, holding the frame for Laura to see.

"That's my favorite." She took the photo and ran her fingers across its surface. "The three brothers. Your grandfather's contemporaries?" The three men in the photo were the original owners of the packaging and shipping plant that Eric had helped redevelop. He used to spend hours with her, lying in bed, romanticizing stories from the past. She smiled as she thought of those nights.

"Great, great grandfather, I think. And I wouldn't be surprised if he knew them. They were all wealthy enough to rub shoulders, I'm sure."

"They were in shipping. Is that what he did?"

"Edward?"

"Your great great whosit."

"Edward," Eric corrected. "The factory owners were packaging. They used Edward Mason for shipping. That's what the tax information said. I thought he might have inherited some more wealth, but that doesn't show up anywhere either."

"Whatever he did, he must have sold his soul to build a palace like that," Laura laughed. "Maybe we could live there someday."

Eric smiled and shook his head. "The museum," he started.

"I know," she finished. "It'll be better preserved."

"And cheaper to maintain. Think of the revenue it could generate for this little town. They'll build us a statue to celebrate. Hell, they might even be able to create a tourist destination out of it. Can you picture it? We get rid of those hideous servants' homes along the sides and replace them with cozy little cabins. People would pay out the nose to stay there. You met that little girl next door, right? You said she plays up there sometimes. Once it's developed, her mother won't have to worry about it anymore."

"And we can move on again," She sighed. Eric would find another project. They would pack up twenty boxes of books again and move on to another town.

Eric sat down at the table and opened his computer. She shouldn't have gotten him started.

"Again?" Laura asked. She was leaning over the table as she kissed him.

Eric smiled, but his long fingers kept tapping at the keyboard. "You'll thank me when it's done. You know this is the worst part of the job, but the paperwork needs to be submitted if we're going to get started on the restoration." He typed another line as Laura sunk into her chair. She was glaring at the piles of paper scattered across the table. "I'll clean it up once everything's done," he added. "You'll wake up to a clean table, I promise." He looked up from the screen and winked at her.

Laura smiled. "I didn't say anything about the mess."

"You didn't have to."

Laura stood and walked out of the kitchen. "I'll see you in bed?"

"I'll be late. Don't wait up."

She hadn't planned to. The majority of the boxes were still stacked in the basement and, if they weren't getting unpacked tomorrow, they would stay in storage for the rest of their time here. She didn't mind keeping all of Eric's books in storage, but the thought of having to unpack everything again made her head throb.

It had always been Eric's job to fill out the paperwork, design the media kits, and to handle the accounting. All of that happened before the partial demolitions started.

She had only just met the neighbors. Laura hadn't even visited the local church yet. Once she got to know the pastor, she'd have a better understanding of the whole community. That's how it happened. In the last two towns, the church charity and development committees had raised the majority of the funds for the restoration. Laura had joined the congregations in order to worship and, by the grace of God, the communities had rallied around her both times. She and Eric had rebuilt history, revitalized a whole city block. It was what they could offer. God blessed everyone with a gift. This was hers. She loved the work. Still, she wondered if the struggle forced too much pressure on their marriage. She had mentioned it to Father Jacob, the pastor at the church in the last town, but he reminded her that duty was a virtue. Her family, he said, was blessed in this area.

Father Jacob had been a blessing himself. It had been his work that provided the small feast for her and Eric after their first Sunday service. He spoke with her each week after office hours had ended. When she first mentioned her intention of developing the factory, he had jumped to life immediately, organizing the stewardship community from within the congregation and ensuring the success of the whole project.

Back then, Laura thought they might make a real home in the community. The congregation had been so helpful. The factory job finished without any major issues. The town held a small festival to celebrate the re-opening. Only after everything quieted, after she found out that they were going to be parents, did Eric mention the next project.

He had been working nights back then, finalizing details and closing the small office. The news surprised her. He had found their next project. Another house in another town had spent the last few decades falling into ruin. He had paused after that, grinning that wide grin, and then added an important note. An inarguable note. A note that stopped her from trying to talk him out of another move and another town. This house was his family's house. His own grandfather had built it, a tribute to his family. Eric had heard stories years ago and only just rediscovered it. Together, they could build it into something useful.

So, she pulled back the covers and laid in bed alone. She wouldn't see him again tonight, not while there was still work to be done. The table would still be covered with papers tomorrow. The boxes would stay in the basement, but the project would launch on time. They would visit the site. They would review and demolish, renovate and restore. History, Eric often said, should be celebrated. Communities, Laura often responded, are built by those who stay.

***

"Did you know that in a lot of places around the world, people use graveyards like we use parks?" Julie tugged at Lacy's apron as she asked. "They play soccer and have picnics and walk their dogs and everything. Have you ever had a picnic in a graveyard? Can we have a picnic on Grandma's grave? You think she'd want us to make scones? What kind of scones should we make?"

Lacy tousled her hair, forgetting for a moment that both of her hands were still covered in flour. Every time another family joined the parish, Lacy stormed into a baking frenzy. Three more pies, then she could take Julie out for a walk. Until then, her focus was the dough at hand. "Sorry kiddo, could you go wash up?"

"I'm going to fix up a picnic basket," Julie continued. "Can I use the cutting board? I'll be extra, extra careful."

"Go wash your hair," Lacy repeated as she pulled out the flour-coated measuring cup. "We can make sandwiches later."

Lacy wanted to drop off at least one of the pies to the new neighbors, Eric and Laura, in person. When they had stopped by a few weeks ago, checking out the small two-bedroom house next to her own, she had made it a point to welcome them with unobtrusive small talk. She was good at making people comfortable in conversation. Everybody said so. She had mentioned how much she liked the little house. They had smiled at each other, then. Lacy remembered how happy the young mother looked. It reminded her of when Julie was born. That was around the same time she moved into her own house. She kneaded the dough and started laying it out across the pie tin as Julie darted past her again, flour still escaping from her hair in puffs.

"Sandwiches!" Julie yelled as she ran out of the kitchen. She let the screen door slam behind her.

"Come back and wash that out of your hair," Lacy called out the window. "Don't go running off. Julie!"

***

After running out of her mother's kitchen with flour in her hair, Julie tumbled down a hill, bolted across a field, and started walking up the old gravel road. She had visited the house before. She had seen the locked gate at the end of the driveway, the one with the faded orange sign. A year ago, that had been enough to make her heart race. She had made out the words on the sign on the first day, letter by letter, but that was forever ago.

Now, the sign was just a sign. It was no reason not to explore. Her mother might not want to admit it, but Julie knew that ten-year-olds were big enough to hike and swim and climb all by themselves. She slipped past the gate and skipped down the long driveway. There, behind the fountain, was the same beautiful house that she had explored almost every weekend since she first mustered up the courage to explore. Back then, she thought her mother's house was fine. She loved swinging from the rope on the big tree in the back yard and helping with the little garden.

This house was nothing like that one. Here, stone towers dwarfed even the nearby trees. Julie wondered what it would be like to live in one of those towers. She thought about Rapunzel and the man who climbed up her hair. Julie didn't want anyone climbing up her hair. She had played at the base of each one of the towers and all of them made her think of living inside. She had walked around and around the house, but no doors would open. It didn't bother her, not one bit. She could stay outside and have just as many adventures. There was an orchard around back. She could pick apples and throw them against the tall stone walls. Maybe she could find an entrance to the basement. Her mother's house had a cellar door that went right into the ground. Maybe there would be a cellar door here too.

Julie walked around the side of the towering building, touching stones and picking wildflowers as she walked. Near the back, she found a small inlet, one she had never seen before, just big enough for her small frame. She turned her head and flattened her body as much as she could. Then, she squeezed through the crevice.

The passage was only a few feet long. Julie struggled, then stumbled out the other side into an unkempt hedge. It pricked at her shirt and caught on her shoelace, but she managed to break free. As she looked around, she saw that she was in the center of a small garden. A single tree stood in the center, surrounded by a circle of cobbled bricks. There were two benches, barely visible beneath the bramble of weeds tangled around them. But, the most striking thing about the garden was the angels.

The whole garden was only the size of their backyard, but there must have been a dozen beautiful stone angels all around her. Some stood with swords in their hands. Others sat near the outer edges, propped up on their unmoving arms. Julie brushed her fingers against one. The stone face was smooth and cold. She sat down next to another and studied its face.

"You're pretty," Julie said. She leaned back, mimicking the angel's pose. "Do you like poetry? My mom told me one about angels. Do you know it?"

When there was no answer, she jumped to her feet, burst into a run, and tripped. Something snapped. Julie landed hard. The palms of her hands scraped on the rough bricks near the tree and she cried out from the sharp pain. Her knee bled. She wiped away the blood, then wiped away her tears.

When she looked up, she was alone in the garden.

All the angels were gone.

***

Eric showed Laura the enormous iron gate and the small footpath around the side.

"Think of the parties we could have here," she said. Eric kept walking. He showed her the empty fountain, the branch that had knocked him over, and the mythical sculptures on the heavy wooden doors. Together, they circled the entire perimeter of the house, checking windows and doors for an open entrance. Instead, they found a whole wing with a collapsed roof, a short tower guarded by stone angels, and an intimate orchard of apple trees near the rear of the house.

"It's funny," Eric said. "I thought there were more statues around the property when I came here earlier." He stopped and closed his eyes, "Pray o' angels, come and stay, lest we ever go astray. Keep all children safe today."

"Never, never go away," Laura finished. Eric used to sing it as a lullaby, tickling her as he sang the last note.

There were alcoves along the stone walls, places that could have displayed life-sized statues. Only the center of the five alcoves displayed a statue, a man in turn-of-the-century attire.

"Edward Mason," Laura read from the stone inscription. "He looks just like you."

"What about the rest?" Eric asked.

"They don't look like anything." Laura smiled at the empty platforms.

"Less to salvage, I guess." Eric kicked at the base of one of the alcoves, knocking a hunk of cracked stone to the ground. "Let's keep looking . . ." His voice trailed off as the breeze picked up.

Some of the stained glass windows on the sides had been shattered, but none were fully destroyed. Eric checked to see if they were all bolted shut and was surprised to find that the only unsecured windows were those on either side of the wooden doors at the front. He pushed one of the tall windows open and, grasping vines and stone to support his tall frame, climbed inside.

He leaned back out and carefully lifted Laura in behind him. "Look at the detail," Laura said as she gazed around the hall. The marble floors were covered in dust, but otherwise uncluttered. A grand staircase loomed over the rest of the hall, stretching toward them like a waterfall of carpeted steps. The banisters circled and looped at the bottom and again at the top. She poked Eric and pointed to the second floor balcony. "It's almost like an old cinema palace. Look at the red carpeting. The decorated ceiling."

"Hello!" Eric tilted his head back as he called out. A soft response echoed. "I'm heading east," Eric said as he wandered off. "You take west."

Laura folded her arms across her chest and examined the painted ceiling. The stars formed constellations. She traced Orion with her pointer finger. The air was cold. She walked west through a broken door, down a hall and, through an entrance to an enclosed garden. There, everything was overgrown. Even the stone benches were covered in moss. She stepped onto the cobbled path and closed her eyes. Climbing ivy and outstretched branches wrapped the edges of the garden, protecting the small space with a thorny embrace. She listened to the wind brush leaves across the ground. The church in Middleport had the same smell. Wet leaves and distant wood-fires. She and Eric had joked about adding a cologne with the same smell to the shop in the updated church lobby. They would name it after Father Jacob. That was two months ago, a lifetime. She imagined waking up to the smell.

Laura felt the goosebumps rise as a breeze bit her flesh. The walls stood, covered in ivy, relics of a different time. She rubbed her hands against her upper arms. She looked behind the tree, stepping on leaves until a stick snapped beneath her foot. She cringed. This wasn't the way she had planned to spend the afternoon. The rest of their own house needed unpacking.

"Come on," she yelled, walking back toward the main hall. "I'm leaving."

There was no response.

***

As Laura called, Eric continued exploring. He walked another hallway in the opposite wing, peeking into each room before checking the next door. He stepped into a study, an empty room, and finally up a spiral stairway to the attic. He squinted in the darkness.

"What are you doing up here?" A voice asked, ringing through the cavernous attic.

Eric spun on his heels. Behind him stood a small girl, half his size, in a tailored red gown and a sparkling silver tiara. He took a deep breath.

"What are you doing up here?" The child repeated. "The party is downstairs."

Eric nodded. Soft music echoed in his ears. The party was

downstairs, after all. He must have been looking for a place to close his eyes for a while. "Just got turned around," he explained. "I've never been here before."

"It's a beautiful house, sir," the girl said. "There's no other place like it in the world."

Eric nodded. He rubbed his eyes.

"Come and see." The girl in the red gown put a hand on Eric's back and led him out of the room, down the stairs, through the hall, and to the gallery with the grand staircase. At the bottom of the grand staircase, she finally let go. When he looked back, she was gone. A tall man, in a dusty black suit, stood in her place.

Edward was a mirror image of the statue outside. His hair was dust. Age caked across his face in layers of wrinkled skin. His jowls sagged. His tall forehead shone with a long, bright reflection, lit by the flame from the candle he held. His hands shook.

"At last," said the man. In a heartbeat, his face twisted and reformed. His hair cropped into a messy black pile atop his head. His back straightened. His suit darkened. Eric saw himself in this new man, this old man. They shared the same stature, the same spindly arms. He stood next to Eric, looking out over the room with a tight frown on his face. "My recent guests simply refused to leave. I was starting to think I might never see the end of them."

Eric nodded. His head was swimming. He thought of the attic and the spirals of stairs that they took back down to the main hall. The girl had mentioned a party. Instead, the room looked just as it had when he and Laura had separated earlier in the evening.

"I knew they would be trouble. Uninvited guests always outstay their welcome." He clapped Eric on the shoulder. "I had nearly abandoned all hope, yet in you climbed. You and that beautiful wife of yours."

"Thank you," Eric said, "but I'm not entirely sure why I'm here. I apologize for the unusual entry. The house was empty. We are going to build a museum here."

"My boy," he motioned across the enormous room with his free arm, "this is no museum. No, this was built for a family."

"It will finally be usable again." Eric covered his mouth with his hand and yawned. When he opened his eyes, he surveyed the room. Now, a piano played. Elaborate chandeliers lit the room. Polished marble fawns groped tall candelabras. The light from their candles danced across immaculate, paper-covered walls. Ten young children, standing near the edges of the room, flipped palm fans to the rhythm of the music. Eric's eyes were heavy.

"The unwelcome guests felt the same way."

"They're gone now?" His whole body ached. He wanted to lay down.

"Gone forever."

"And we should settle down."

"As soon as you'd like."

The iron chandelier in the center of the ceiling hung low, casting flickers of light across the entire room. Shadows emerged and retreated in every corner. Eric wanted to curl up in those shadows, but the man was staring at him. Eric smiled weakly. "What changed? The visitors, I mean. They've left?"

A snarl fell into the man's face. "We built our house as strong as stone, but never do devils dance alone."

"Until an heir reclaims the throne," Eric continued.

"Then blood for blood and bone for bone." The shadows in the room grew larger. "What do you know of blood?"

Eric gave no answer. Edward held the candle in front of him as he walked toward the back of the hall, behind and beneath the grand staircase. Eric followed. They stopped in front of a mural that took up the entire underside of the stairs. Eric studied the landscape, tall pines against a stormy sky. In the center of the painting, a stone fountain stood in the middle of a dirt driveway. "The estate," Eric said. "Only there's no castle in the painting. There are gardens. And statues."

"It's a warning. Your father once imagined this little horror. He would have allowed the house to fall into ruins. You, of course, considered the same outcome. But we can't allow that, not now. You've seen the beauty here. You, like me, would do anything to prevent the destruction of such a family heirloom. And so might your son, when his time comes."

Eric's focus blurred as he studied the painting. Shadows danced across the walls. He did want to prevent the destruction of this beautiful place. He wanted to settle down with Laura. He wanted to watch his son grow up. He wanted to build this museum. He wanted to tear down this house. He forced his eyes back open. The room was empty again.

As Eric stepped back from the wall where the painting had hung, the whole room groaned. "Laura . . " Eric started, but his voice cracked. Weariness swallowed him again. When he turned to leave, the room melted into golden tapestries and silver platters. Candles glittered on every surface. Couples in formal attire danced across the room. Wild notes howled a siren's song from an unseen orchestra.

"Your darling wife, bless her soul, can stay as long as she likes," Edward said as he guided Eric to the grand staircase. "There's just one more step and everything will be set."

***

Laura landed on the wet soil outside the window. She brushed off her knees. There, ahead of her, stood a small figure in the center of the path. A child. The small figure walked in short steps, her steps muffled. The crunch of gravel below Laura's own feet were shouts in the quiet night air.

"Julie?" Laura called out. She recognized the girl's face. She had met Julie before, back before they bought the little house. The neighbor had come by with her little daughter whizzing around the yard behind her. The girl looked different now. Her eyes were sullen and her skin pale in the moonlight. Her movements were slow. If Julie had been a storm, she was now a mist.

"I'm sorry," the little girl said, "but you can't go just yet."

Laura squinted, trying to decide if the girl was ill or playing a game. "Does Lacy know you're up here all alone? Give me your hand. We can walk out together."

"We aren't alone," the girl said. She walked to Laura and held out her hand. Laura grasped it. The hand was cold, as if Julie had been standing outside for hours. "Your husband and I have reached an agreement. Please, accept my humble invitation." The little girl led them back toward the house.

"Eric?" Laura asked. "Did you see Eric?"

The girl stopped at the fountain and pointed up toward the nearest tower. Laura could see a man standing on the ledge of the highest window. As she parted her lips to ask, she realized who it was. The man held out one foot, then tipped forward. Laura watched Eric careen face-first into the hard stone stairs leading up to the door. The little girl gripped Laura's hand tightly. They both screamed as he smashed to the ground. Laura fell to her knees. Julie wrapped her arms around Laura's head and pulled her close.

"The angels are gone," the little girl explained. "This is our house again."

Laura pulled away from the tiny cold hands and watched, through her tears, as the girl's face contorted like a mess of wet clay.

"Finally," the girl with Eric's face continued, "we're home."

The End.

Case #57241

Jim Markus

Jim Markus lives in Chicago, Illinois. He is the author of Write with Lions. His work is often featured on MoreKnown.com.

CLAYTON HILL SANITARIUM

CLAYTON HILL SANITARIUM

A Very White and Scarlet Christmas

Luke Tarzian

Physician: Dr. Peterson
8268-WCT29

21

It was Christmas morning, just a quarter past midnight. The snow fell lightly from the gray and black above, and frost hung heavy on the trees. Jimmy crouched inside the bushes, stroking furiously, trying to contain his gasps of pleasure, as watched all five feet, seven inches of Amy Donahue undress.

"Yeah baby...nice and slow....just like that," he whispered as she slid her skirt and leggings off. He went a little faster, smiling excitedly, trying to prevent his breath from fogging up the window, as she undid the buttons on her scarlet blouse, singing to the radio.

He sees you when you're sleeping—

"Oh yeah I do...."

He knows when you're awake—

"Mhmm..."

He knows when you you've been bad or good, so be good for goodness sake—

"But I like it when you're naughty, baby—please don't stop...."

Jimmy's hand went faster as he watched her stretch, captivated by the smoothness of her creamy skin, the graceful arching of back, the way her auburn hair bounced freely, and the way her nipples perked up in the cold. He started shaking as he neared his climax.

"Nice and slow baby—rub the lotion nice and slow—all along those legs...and just pretend that's my—"

And then he heard a jingle, faint at first, but then quite near. Just as Jimmy was about to finish he was taken out by force, knocked over on his side, pants around his ankles, cock in hand, laying baffled in the snow. He looked up just in time to see a giant figure in a red suit, wearing black boots, flanked by deer-like creatures and a sled.

"You've been a very naughty boy this year, Jimmy."

And then the figure brought his boot down repeatedly on Jimmy's face until it was a mass of gore and fragments of his skull and spattered brain. He called the deer-like creatures with a clicking of his teeth:

"Meal time boys—and take your time." He looked in the window, grinning wide and bulging as the woman sprawled out naked on her bed, still singing as she started pleasuring herself. "Ho ho ho...Amy Donahue, you've been a very naughty girl this year. Let's see what Santa has for you inside his sack."

And then he sauntered to the front door and began to pick the lock.

The End.

Case #15780

Luke Tarzian

Luke was born in Bucharest, Romania in 1990 and has been writing since 2005. He's a graduate of the California State University of Fullerton, with a B.A. in English. He's an aspiring novelist, artist, a lover of cats, and likes to indulge in a nice Jack and Coke every now and then. He firmly believes that Grumpy Cat is his soul animal. He's influenced by a plethora of writers, most notably Edgar Allan Poe and H.P. Lovecraft, and is currently working on the second book in his "Sewn From Seeds" trilogy. His work has appeared in several issues of Sanitarium Magazine and his Dracula origin story, Durante Lucus, was recently sold to Alban Lake's Blood Bond imprint.

http://luketarzian.wordpress.com
http://facebook.com/rowesofficial
http://twitter.com/luke_tarzian

CLAYTON HILL SANITARIUM

CLAYTON HILL SANITARIUM

Ft. Tipii

Deborah Palmer

Physician: Dr. Edgar
9828-SJE41

27

couldn't build a proper tree house. Too high up and anyway I'm afraid of heights, so instead I built this little fort of sorts as a place to gather my thoughts after a hectic day. Made my best efforts with whatever materials the forest floor offered up as building materials. There were enough twigs and branches to construct more ground level tree houses or make my current enclosure larger but I chose to save some for kindling for warmth against the chill night air and the rest I kept stacked as a type of cord-wood in a womb like nook Mother Nature had carved into a tree that had been struck by lightning. Eventually I decided to construct another Tipii twig abode to store my few belongings I had gradually begun to sneak away from The Family Residence.

These Tree/Tepee/Tipii/Twig aka T3 structures became my holy sanctuaries and safe havens I return to again and again to re-connect with Mother Earth and nature. Too small to stand upright clicking my heels together three times was not an option so I was forced to remain seated. With some degree of discomfort I could lay down in a fetal position while I imagined myself re-entering an alternate womb to be reborn into better circumstances. Mine were a tepee shelters without the buffalo skin covering all exposed bones and framework.

Tipii-Hut

Sometimes I'd hug my knees and rhythmically rock back and forth while repeating what I thought were calming mantras, occasionally wishing that the earth would open up and swallow me whole transporting me some place free from pain, misery and cruelty. Like a shaman I chanted using my homemade rituals attempting to silence the drumbeat of voices incessantly chattering inside my head versus the declarations of the Family. They created a dissonance tear in the time frame continuum of my thoughts.

You see our house, The Family Home if you could call it that is a ramshackle structure; a hodgepodge mixture of stone, wood and stucco additions and afterthoughts as different parts of the building were constructed at different times upon the whims the directors and caretakers.

I was forced to share this mishmash cottage with twelve other inmates, bordered on this expanse of woods providing me a refuge from leaky roofs, busted walls, peeling wallpaper, lukewarm baths, moldy musty scented showers, not to mention all the yelling, screaming, arguments, fights, thefts of food and personal belongings and constant disagreements of a house too small to accommodate the number of people residing within its creaky ramparts. The Family nicknamed it the Hotel California. You know the place where you check in but never check out. The nails across chalkboard voices of The Family were constant knife thrusts to my brain making daily life a constant battle that did not end even has the diurnal gave up residence to the nocturnal for they all snored, wheezed and gasped through the night abyss. The utter desolation of the place crept into your bones and took root nourished by hopelessness.

The Family's house sits on an oddly place piece of land, our house gives way to forest which in turn after several miles gives way to craggy, rocky shores of a steep cliff, where if one sits perfectly still you can hear the violent waves crashing against rough jagged rock formations that looked as though they were designed by the devil himself. It is said that in olden times there used to be many shipwrecks where sailors were either impaled on the razor sharp Stalagmites. Sometimes you can even hear the shrieks, moans, cries and groans of the unfortunate wretches mixed in with the howling winds. The few who weren't dashed to pieces by the razor sharp jagged rock formations tried to climb up to safety but were thwarted by the steep incline.

Forest Hiding Place

So I periodically retreated to my exoskeleton asylums as a sentry medium between earth and sky. I can never turn my mind off completely but within my secret hiding place the voices were kept to a low roar and bid to change direction and pace.

The last straw that broke the camel's back came when my moronic addled brained cell-mate Pearl kept throwing her nasty, dirty towels, underwear and flip-flops over to my side of the room. When I returned from the canteen or our common dining area there were moldy wet towels plastered to the floor like throw rugs that accosted the dividing line between our two living areas. Pearl was known as the filthiest female in our wing tossing food and drink to and fro fully expecting that a squad of personal maids and sweepers were following in her wake. One night after I returned from my many woodland sojourns I decided that I had, had enough and soaked all her grimy towels in gasoline and lighter fluid obtained from an unlocked supply closet near the motor pool. Pearl had a tendency to drink like sailor on shore leave and sleep just as soundly so she never had an inkling as I piled the towels around her bed, built a kindling fort for good measure and added effect, led a fuse from a doorway to an open window, climbed out and lit said fuse.

The Kindling delivered me from The Family's vocalizations. I tried to warn them before. I tried to silence the voices through escape, but it was not working so I had to try another plan. The crackles and pops of my campfire seem to be in sync with the screams and cries for rescue from the patients locked inside their rooms but eventually those voices will die out also, and then sleep. Blessed sleep.

Love,

Cassandra Verity

Case #62453

Deborah Palmer

Born in 1959, in the Bronx, New York and raised in St. Albans, Queens, now living in Brooklyn, NY. Served in the US Army from 1977 – 1981. I received my BA in English from Marymount Manhattan College in 2002. Currently I work for the Metropolitan Museum of Art.

My primary love resides with poetry but I have embraced both short stories and searing commentary with open arms. I'm currently working on a memoir for my mother Mable Palmer and a book of romance poems.

Website: Espiritu en Fuego
http://dancingpalmtrees.wordpress.com
Email: deborah.palmer280@gmail.com

Twitter
@Dancingpalmtree
Writer, Educator, Researcher, avid book reader and Tattoo enthusiast
http://twitter.com/dancingpalmtree

CLAYTON HILL SANITARIUM

CLAYTON HILL SANITARIUM
My Own Hero
Kim Culpepper
Physician: Dr. Lotherton
8715-AED19
33

I came of age in a time of no heroes. Not one of them was willing to stand up to the horde as they devoured the human population one by one. Fear killed the hope of every living human being that attempted to survive in the world of the undead. I decided to be the hero in my own world when I was fourteen, watching as my parents were helplessly consumed by the evil masses. I decided to be the hero in my own life, when they weren't there to protect me anymore.

Finding food and shelter proved to be more difficult than usual as I had no sense of what nourishment was. I would run from empty store to empty gas station, cherishing every piece of candy and warm soda that I could find. The lack of protein hit me hard as I fell to the floor of a drug store just outside of Birmingham, Alabama. That's when I first saw him.

He was standing over me, slightly pushing me in the side with his size 9 steel toe boot. The smell of rotten flesh and body odor hit me like smelling salts. I looked over to see he had fought and fought well. The smears of black blood and red handprint covered his pants and his boots, which had once been brown, were now a manly shade of pink.

"You alive?" his husky voice sounded at me.

I let out a moan that was supposed to say yes but, ended up sounding more like a moan from the dead. I felt the stained blade at my neck as he contemplated a swift hack against it.

"Speak now or forever hold your piece little one." he said.

"I'm alive!" I yelled out angrily.

He removed the blade from my neck and stepped away slowly before pulling out a piece of beef jerky from a black book bag he carried on his shoulders. He placed it down onto my lips and I chewed feverishly. I quickly found my senses and was able to look intently at the man who had found me.

He was a short man that looked like the apocalypse had aged him years. If I had to guess, I would say he was sixty but, I knew quickly that he was holding onto his forties. He helped me up off of the drug store floor when we heard the moaning from the back stockroom. We weren't alone anymore. They had found us.

Two stock boys came out from the back, green aprons still on as if they were still slave to some dream that would never be.

They moaned at us and my savior raised his machete up, ready to administer permanent death to them both. I admired him as he took them out, quickly and mercilessly.

He rubbed the black blood that came from within them onto his green and black army pants and reached out a hand for me to shake. It was old and dry and hadn't seen soap and water in what seemed like months. I looked at it and he dropped it down to his side.

"You're not much for human interaction are ya?" he asked with his obvious Southern accent. It annoyed me slightly as he sounded stupid with every word.

"I don't keep company with strangers." I said as I walked away from him, my trusty metal baseball bat in tow.

"Hey! I just saved your life and you can't be no older than twelve."

I stopped at his blatant insult to my age and lowered my head, attempting to control my anger. He had just saved my life yet he was already annoying me.

"I'm fourteen." I said through gritted teeth.

"Well excuse me little missy."

I continued to walk forward at his small apology when he grabbed me by the arm. I felt my face go red and my inhibitions flew away from me. I rubbed the tip of the pistol that my dad had given before he died just for 'last resorts'.

"I just wanted some company. I saw you layin there and I thought we could be friends." he said.

I had yet to turn around and he had let go of my arm.

I turned to look at his innocent looking face and knew that he meant well.

"Are you trying to be a hero?" I asked him through empty eyes.

"Well yea. You're young. You probably need a superhero." he said as he took the expected superhero pose that I use to look through in my dad's used comic books while we were on the road to God knew where trying to escape the epidemic that would prove to be inescapable.

I pulled the pistol from my pocket and pointed it at his child-like face. He held his hands up in surrender.

"Whoa, little one. I don't mean no harm."

His disrespect to my age had reached a boiling point as I pulled the trigger and watched his body fall the floor. The bullet had traveled straight to his forehead and exited into the wall behind him, along with his brains.

I replaced the pistol into my pocket and grabbed what was left of the beef jerky from the front registers of the drug store. I smiled as I exited, proving to myself that I was the hero in my own story and nobody else would be.

The End.

Case #48063

Kim Culpepper

A native of Columbus, MS and married with 2 kids and 2 cats, Kim Culpepper's work has appeared on Books of the Dead Press's blog, The Opening Line Literary Zine, on horror-writers.net, writer.ly, and on Pen and Muse blog. Her debut novel, The Blood Talisman, will be self published in January 2014. You can follow her on Twitter @kculpepper1 or check out her website kjculpepper.net.

CLAYTON HILL SANITARIUM

CLAYTON HILL SANITARIUM

Black Mere

Paul Michael Moreau

Physician: Dr. Lichten
6428-SED41

37

Across the field behind the church Black Mere broods unseen beneath the cold star bright sky. Thin mist rolls past as if released from its depths to carry secrets long submerged. Enduring truths rise as spectres--ancient axioms that make me a killer.

I have stood by the church for two hours in the chill March night before finally I resign to give up my vigil and snatch some fitful sleep before dawn. At that exact moment, I see a dark rounded shape moving along the wall between churchyard and field.

Cold fear thrusts an irrational hand into my stomach when this too tangible visitant turns towards me. I am ready to run out in to Two Gate Lane and home to the village a quarter of a mile distant but I steel myself, determined to look, relieved when its approach resolves into a short, elderly woman in tatty overcoat and woollen hat, just flesh and blood, nothing to fear.

"You'll not see her tonight though I fancy she's not far away." I recognise Miss Gurney, an eccentric spinster living in a caravan on the far side of the mere. How did she know what I waited for? For how many nights has she watched me standing here?

"You know about her?"

"With certainty, since you first saw her my dear." She looked around at the headstones sniffing the cold night air. "Although I must say I've felt her presence for a while longer."

"Have there been sightings in the past?"

"Not in my lifetime though I thought you might realise the truth of the matter by now: it's not the churchyard she's haunting, it's you."

***

Barford St. Andrew felt like home from the moment we arrived: an hour's drive from my new job, the house of our dreams, and a great school though Vicky felt the wrench of leaving the south coast. The village possessed timeless charm, welcoming and familiar, half-remembered and offering a fresh start under the vast East Anglian sky.

I first saw her one night in January when taking a shortcut home from the pub out on the main road, the same spot where I once watched a glowing ball of light moving low across the field behind the church. Faint translucence took on substance until I looked upon a young woman with sad glistening eyes framed by wild hair, barefoot and clad in a simple white dress.

She faded within seconds leaving only old graves amid wells of deep shadow. I heard a cry, distant and indistinct but the wind whispered in the treetops and I could not be certain.

Struck by her fleeting beauty I began haunting the churchyard myself most nights hoping to see her again, unafraid despite her obvious nature. Vicky deplored my increasingly erratic behaviour, the problems at work, mood swings, and drinking. She resented the long hours I spent out, said I neglected the kids by not being there for them, no longer reading bedtime stories. What could I tell her? That I was seeing another woman but it is OK, she is only a ghost?

Most evenings I took only the moon and stars for company, often staying out past midnight. The occasional car passed through the village, its lingering approach and departure clearly audible in the still night, dogs barked on distant farms and the wind spoke but the girl did not reappear. I saw the corpse light again, gliding very slowly towards me from the mere but it receded rapidly, becoming smaller and ultimately vanishing as I walked to meet it.

Winter wore on, my life unravelling further due to fatigue. Vicky and I now slept in separate rooms when I slept at all. The girl returned in the small hours one brittle night, just the briefest glimpse but undoubtedly her. She stood by the churchyard wall eyes filled with terror, body frozen in an attitude of desperate entreaty as she dissolved into nothingness.

***

Miss Gurney studies my face as if seeking the answer to some puzzle.

"I'm David, David Stratton," I say.

"I know that dear, it's a small village." She shivers and pulls her coat tighter. "Walk me back to my caravan and we'll see if we can make some sense out of all this."

The narrow lane twists and climbs its way around the mere with little more than the hedgerow separating us from the cold water. Stars shine like lanterns as frost creeps over bare fields.

For as long as anyone remembered Miss Gurney's makeshift home has been a fenced-off field corner half a mile or so from the family farm, a quiet sanctuary of vegetable plots, fruit bushes, and cats. Her old showman's caravan is just visible from the lane beyond the chaotic tangle of brambles forming her unkempt border. All the local children think she is a witch.

She left me to my thoughts, glancing up now and then with a gleam in her eye. At her gate, she fixed me with a steely gaze saying:

"That land by the mere has always been sacred ground, long before the first church was built. Do you realise how long the past maintains its grip in certain places? Longer than you might think and here, where the old religion persisted until the seventh century, it has a particularly long reach."

"Who is she?"

"Just some poor wretch who cannot let go of this world, with a connection to you of course or rather to your subconscious, some unfinished business."

"I'd never been to Norfolk before we moved into the village."

"I'm talking about previous lives; I sense this poor creature has been waiting such a long time and you hold the key to her release. There's a winter connection too."

She is quite barmy, a harmless eccentric but I have doubts about telling her how I have felt since the first sighting, that hollow feeling, a sense of some forgotten yearning I am unable to satisfy, but she inexplicably knows it all anyway. Some instinct bid her come to me in the churchyard.

"I'm not sure I'm ready to believe in reincarnation but thanks for your concern."

"Think about what I have said." She spoke softly but with a stern tone like an old-fashioned schoolmistress. "Should you care to visit me I can take you back so as to put right whatever troubles you and put a finish to it. Goodnight David."

***

I spent less time at the church as a new obsession held sway, plunging instead into the history of the village and surrounding country. At weekends, I plagued every bookshop for miles around, revisiting the march of past ages: the diggers of flint, the first farmers and men of iron, the pre-Christian ways of Celt and Roman, Saxon and Dane. I saw the annual cycle through their eyes, understanding their dependence on unknown forces governing the cycle of change, the fertility of the land. I learned of the fear manifest in the giant Wandil, he who threatened to steal away and swallow the unborn spring, leaving only eternal winter. He the gods cast into the heavens where his fiery eyes still shine and the long black nights are his gaping maw as he brings ice and snow to cover the land.

The new season required offerings of the people: small tokens such as jewellery or coin in good years, cattle or other livestock in harder ones. Only in the harshest of times, when winter reigned long and food stocks ran low, might the ultimate supplication prove necessary to ensure renewal of the annual miracle: the springing to life of precious seeds and a good harvest.

The old ways survive in the lore of festive dates, in beliefs of potion and cure, in the fearing of spells cast by witches or cunning men. They persist in the wearing of good luck charms or those votive offerings still occasionally found in secret wild places. The long winter nights still lay heavy upon scattered farms and hamlets as they wait the season's turn.

With my mind so attuned, my imagination conjured every possibility, sane or otherwise. I remained sceptical of the old woman's assertion that she could help yet a fortnight later I walked up after dark, pushing my way along her overgrown path.

***

Curtained windows glow and smoke swirls from the chimney. Before I can knock Miss Gurney opens the caravan door, beckoning me in with a half-whisper:

"Ah! There you are David, I've been expecting you."

"I'm going to take up your offer; I want to understand what is happening to me." I climbed the steps and Miss Gurney shut the door behind us with a satisfied smile.

Her caravan is surprisingly roomy and lit by oil lamps. A large ginger cat leaps indignantly to the floor as I sit on a padded bench. Miss Gurney remains in the kitchen area close by the door with her black cat fussing about her ankles.

"It's so much cosier than living in the big house. I could never do that nowadays and they must cost a fortune to run. Have you seen her again?" She strikes a match, lighting the gas hob and setting a copper kettle upon the ring.

"No, but I've been thinking about what you said. I won't say I'm convinced but I'd like to give it a try, resolve this while I still have a career and marriage."

"I think it's the mere you know, that's what connects you to her just as the present remains attached to the past. I'll tell you a story only known within the family.

"My father used to fly; long before I was born he owned one of the first private aircraft in Norfolk, something very special in those days. He went up one morning in July 1914 making several circuits around farm and village. Looking down at the mere on the last run, he saw the face of a beautiful girl with an expression of absolute sorrow looking up from its surface. He was quite definite about it, always claiming some intimation of the coming war but I wonder about that now."

The kettle boils and she takes a pestle and mortar from the cupboard, grinding away before adding the contents to an old enamel mug. A curious smell, something infuriatingly familiar, pervades the caravan as the water pours.

"What have you brewed there?"

Oh, various roots, bits of this and that. It will make you quite drowsy and then we'll make sense of this strange business."

The drink has a bittersweet taste and I lie on the bench with my eyes closed while Miss Gurney potters about her kitchen.

"Out you go Old Thomas and Mister Sooty." I hear her open the door and shoo out the cats as if in a dream. My eyelids are heavy and I have no sense of time. When I manage to open them briefly, I see her lighting a pair of scented candles. In their flickering light, the caravan begins to distort and swim.

"I'm going to take you back so you can put things right dear. Just lie there and relax."

Lost memories surface--a knife with a deer antler handle, a brooch bearing a white horse. The cold water fringed by trees with a small grove close by, an anomaly in the sparsely wooded agrarian landscape, a hallowed place, our temple.

"See her face clearly in your mind, keep it focussed and let her draw you back."

I can see her now and feel her fear and sorrow. Cruel winds sweep the land of unborn spring. Its fecundity, should it ever come, uncertain in the face of raw primeval forces.

"Relax, breathe gently and..."

***

A thin thread of consciousness, some twisted filament of awareness holds me as I look down on icy water amid a barren landscape. The few trees are rigid with hoarfrost and I recognise my village close by.

Its desperate people shiver in heavy cloaks and sheepskins as they march in grey predawn light. At their head, the priests and attendants surrounding the cart bearing Oona walk in solemn silence.

I remember how I failed her on this day through shameful weakness, hiding myself far away despite her own calm acceptance. As her cart reaches the simple ditch and palisade enclosing the grove, the bronze trumpets blare and this time I take my place amid the throng.

We were together throughout that long terrible winter, fear and desperation our constant companions at the end. As a last resort, the priests cast lots, each virgin girl choosing a portion of sanctified bread. Oona held the marked portion, its underside burnt and blackened, so becoming the one devoted to our salvation.

They kept her apart and we no longer spoke. A well-born girl of just fourteen summers made a most suitable propitiation for the good of all, a surety that the grim one be assuaged.

Yesterday she ate her last meal of precious grain--all the seeds we must plant soon. Then her last journey began, taking her from farm to farm in her guise of goddess, her hand-hauled chariot a simple wicker-sided cart. All night we worshipped her as fires burned and boar-headed carnyces resounded. Dancers strove to awaken the slumbering god who abandoned us.

Now as dawn approaches they lead her to the water's edge, the attendants following close behind, no longer an earthly sister but our gift to the divine. They shave her hair and she shivers because her simple dress is thin but also through fright. Then the dress is stripped away leaving her naked apart from the sacred cord around her neck.

The first glow lights the horizon and the high priest leads her waist deep into to the water. The unforgiving wind blows as the crowd fall silent.

She must go willingly without struggle if the gift is to be accepted yet she cannot help looking back. Her eyes flicker with fear but this time mine are there to meet their gaze and, with a barely perceptible nod of the head, I offer my love.

The priest grasps her throat as the dim sun breaks. The next instant he is pressing her beneath the water, holding her down on her back to drown as the attendants wade in bearing the branches and stones that will keep body and spirit in place. We are all relieved, hope remains in this world and I am proud of her.

***

Things did not work out with Vicky, too much damage done I suppose. She said I was sick, that I needed a doctor. After I lost my job, we put the house on the market and she took the kids back down south. I stayed on, finding casual work and renting a former granny annexe on the edge of the village. I belong here now; nothing would induce me to leave.

I visited Miss Gurney several times a week before she died that December. She taught me everything she knew about the old ways during those precious months and I inherited the notebooks and journals she feared her family might destroy.

The winter was exceptionally hard. Deep snow covered the fields leaving remote villages isolated for weeks. The worst was in February but the long freeze persisted, the bleak east firmly held in Wandil's grasp.

I saw her late one night while out driving, a slip of a girl no more than sixteen, walking along the road in a skirt far too short for the unrelenting cold. Fresh snow fell as I pulled over and lowered the passenger window.

"Missed the last bus?" She look frightened but I smiled "It's OK, I've a daughter of my own, where you heading?"

"Attleborough," she replied, holding her arms across her body, shivering in the raw bite.

"It's pretty much on my way." I opened the door.

She didn't want to talk so I put some music on to lighten the mood and she relaxed a little. I thought of the rope and breezeblocks in the boot.

As I turned off the main road before the village, I gave another reassuring smile, saying:

"I know all the shortcuts."
It was past midnight, a brand new day, snow still lying on the Spring Equinox. I drove slowly along Two Gate Lane towards Black Mere.

The End.

Case #79546

Paul Michael Moreau

Paul Michael Moreau is a former I.T. professional living on the south coast of the United Kingdom and currently writing in various speculative fiction genres. He has been published in weird fiction magazine Morpheus Tales and has stories forthcoming in the Morpheus Tales: Ethereal Tales Special Issue and the Raus! Untoten! anthology series from Fringeworks Ltd.

In addition to short form speculative fiction, current projects include a cycle of sword and sorcery stories (highly unfashionable I know but Howard was pretty much the first genre writer I read after Burroughs and led me to C.L. Moore, Fritz Leiber et al) and an ecological thriller and genre mash-up which will see old forces arise in the modern psyche and the South Downs running red.

Paul writes at a second-floor bay window with a view of a massive Grade 1 listed Victorian church and the sea beyond. He has a nearly completed first draft of an historical novel set amongst the German community on the Texas frontier circa 1875 festering in a shoebox somewhere but is currently having more fun hunting demons in deep space.

CLAYTON HILL SANITARIUM

Bestselling Horror US

1 Doctor Sleep - *Stephen King*

2 Bad Thoughts - *Dave Zeltserman*

3 The Shining - *Stephen King*

4 Finding Christmas - *James Calvin Schaap*

5 The Silence of the Lambs - *Thomas Harris*

6 1/22/63 - *Stephen King*

7 World War Z - *Max Brooks*

8 John Dies at the End - *David Wong*

9 ORBS - *Nicholas Sansbury Smith*

10 NOS4A2 - *Joe Hill*

Compiled November 1st -November 30th 2013
Amazon.com Kindle Chart

Bestselling Horror UK

1. Doctor Sleep - *Stephen King*
2. Bad Thoughts - *RR Haywood*
3. Dead Air (Book One of The Dead Series) - *Jon Schafer*
4. The Shining - *Stephen King*
5. Guarding His Mate (Lycan Romance) - *M L Briers*
6. Arisen, Book Five - EXODUS - *Michael Stephen Fuchs*
7. World War Z - *Max Brooks*
8. *Lastnight (The Jack Nightingale Super)- Stephen Leather (Pre-Order)*
9. HOUSE OF MALICE - *Scott Mariani*
10. Grace (Lycan Romance) - *A. B Lee*

Compiled November 1st -November 30th 2013
Amazon.co.uk Kindle Chart

Group
Therapy
12.13
Did you make the
Naughty or Very Naughty
List this year?
52

The Vampire Queen

This month I did something different. I posted a poll question on facebook to get an insight to my question. Here's the question: "From 1922 to present, who is your favorite person who's played Dracula?" There was overwhelming support for Gary Oldman in his portrayal of Dracula in Bram Stoker's movie Dracula. I was absolutely shocked at the result. My only possible reasoning behind this decision is that Bram Stoker's Dracula was more portrayed as a lover rather than a monster. His love for Mina took over the story. He was given the opportunity to turn the usual Dracula monster story into a love story between Mina and 'Dracula'. He was given the chance to show real emotion and real love for a forbidden consort. Never has Dracula portrayed such depth in their stories so this was a real novelty. Here's a little known fact, Bram Stoker died penniless and his wife had to sell his drawings and short stories to Sotherby's just to survive. He failed to properly copyright Dracula and therefore lost out big on the use of his story.

There was a two vote honorable mention of Bela Lugosi which really surprised me as I thought he'd be the winner. He's been my favorite all these years and even with such Dracula-like characters such as Tom Cruise and Stuart Townsend, Bela is still my favorite. There was just something about this Hungarian man, who spoke no English when he came here, who was fortunate enough to score the roll as the mysterious Dracula. He, too, died penniless as he was never paid well for all his rolls as Dracula and who never knew how to manage American money. Funny the coincidences between Bela and Bram. Too bad he didn't win but he'll always be the favorite in my book.

Keep the questions coming. You can write to me at

thevampirequeensanitariummag@gmail.com with all your vampire/horror questions. I look forward to hearing from you.

Keep Writing!
The Vampire Queen

REVIEWS

Dracula's Midnight Snacks
By David Saunderson
Review by Casey Chapli

I'm at a bit of a crossroads with the review I'm about to write. Usually things are fairly black and white when it comes to whether or not something is good (Good being totally subjective.). But in the case of Dracula's Midnight Snacks, it's just not that simple. The book in question is another anthology, a collection of stories, but all with a common theme - vampires. It's a popular theme in today's fiction, but these stories are nothing like what you would read about in a Stephenie Meyer novel, no they're far more traditional. All of those aspects are very admirable, and quite exciting for somebody who might feel that the vampire mythos has been bastardized.

Now, you might be thinking what could be bad about that? Well, as well written and structured the stories are, as full and finished as many of them may be, I am simply not a fan of the structured writing or the genre in which is being written. When I read something, I prefer a free flowing script rather than the old school style in which most, if not all of the tales are penned. By old school, I mean that very much in a literal sense as well. Reading many of these stories reminded me of Robert Louis Stevenson, or Bram Stoker himself, which in every aspect is a compliment.

Now do you see my confusion about this particular work? I'm stuck between being a fan and a reviewer, which aren't two totally separate things. I can review books and stories because I am a fan and because I myself, am an author. But rarely do I enjoy what I'm reading, all the while feeling like it's a chore, and that is exactly where I was at with Dracula's Midnight Snacks. I feel though that when a situation such as this arises it's best to use an impartial judgement, and with that, I must say that Dracula's Midnight Snacks is a well written, well put together, and a well told collection of stories, especially if you do enjoy the form of writing that might have come out of 1897.

Dracula's Midnight Snacks is filled with wonderment and fantasy, all the while keeping the stories grounded and realistic. It is definitely easy to lose yourself in the Stoker-esque settings and writing, and quite fascinating to read about a time long lost through the imagination of somebody living today. it wasn't easy for me at times to finish the stories, and siding with reason rather than emotion was probably the best way for me to review this work.

So, I do say this collection is worth giving a chance, but do be warned that the style and format may not be for everybody.

VERDICT 81%

About Casey:

Casey Chaplin is a horror writer, reviewer, and content creator. He has written a full length horror novel entitled Lizzy; competed several screenplays for production, and writes reviews for various websites and magazines including Gamers Mantra and Sanitarium Magazine. He has an education in Radio Broadcasting, with a major in Creative Writing and has worked both full time and freelance for several radio stations.

COMPETITION

From the editors at Writer's Digest, this fantastic resource for horro writers details hundreds of magazine and book publishers who are interested in acquiring and publishing new frightful fiction. Each market listing provides information on where the publisher is located, what they're looking for, who to contact, how to reach them, and what their terms are.

Were giving away a KINDLE copy every and every month,. To win all you need to do to enter is email us your name and subject line "horror writer".

horrorwriter@sanitariummagazine.com

The name of the winner will be printed in next months issue. Also it will appear on our website on or just after the 20th of the month.

Keep on writing and good luck!

WINNER:

IAN REEVES

CLAYTON HILL SANITARIUM

Elder's End

Anthony Watson

Physician: Dr. Peterson
8268-WCT29

62

He awoke to birdsong, a cacophony of tweets, twitters, coos and the occasional squawk. He slowly opened his eyes and blinked them to adjust to the artificial twilight created within the tent, a murky greyness of nylon-filtered light. He yawned, expansively, then coughed and spluttered as the cool – no, cold – air filled his lungs.

He shuffled onto his back, the inflatable bed on which his sleeping bag lay squeaking its comedy fart sounds as he did. Once prone, he wriggled within the bag to extricate his arms, awkwardly manoeuvring them out of the snug warmth.

"Good morning world!" He said.

He listened to the avian conversations around him for a few minutes before completing his exit from the sleeping bag, shuffling the tube off his body to lie in a crumpled heap at his feet. Leaning over to the side, he retrieved his clothes – the ones he hadn't actually slept in, shirt and trousers – and pulled them on, wriggling and contorting within the confines of the tent. He slipped his trainers onto his feet, not bothering to tie the laces.

Getting to his knees, he shuffled towards the flap at the bottom of the tent and unzipped it in one sweeping arc. Daylight flooded into the tent – he'd not zipped up the outer flaps and as a result his boots and the various bits of paraphernalia he'd left in the entrance were coated in a layer of dew. Unwilling to get his knees wet, he sat back down and stretched his legs out of the tent and pushed himself forwards, grunting with the exertion. His movements caused one of the guy-ropes on the tent to twang loudly, the vibrating nylon throwing droplets of water into the air.

Finally outside of the tent he stretched, arms upraised, feeling the kinks and knots in his back popping and loosening. He rotated his head, heard the tendons in his neck creak and grind. A quick shake of his shoulders and arms completed his morning warm-up routine.

He'd camped on top of a hill, making the effort the night before to get to the top in anticipation of the view that would greet him this morning. Looking out on the vista that presented itself, he congratulated himself on that decision and took deep breaths of cool, refreshing air.

A low mist clung to the ground in the valley below him, covering everything in a pale white blanket. Hills and undulations poked through this blanket, resembling islands in a white sea. He'd managed to set up the tent so that he would be facing east as he climbed out of it and so have the perfect view of the sun rising, a deep red orb that floated above the ethereal landscape. As he watched, a flock of geese slowly made its way across the sky, a huge V-shape from which a chorus of honks arose, clearly audible even at this distance, the birds flying back here to spend the winter in warmer climes.

Music filled his head, a familiar theme though one whose name he didn't know. The Rites of Spring? Maybe. Pastoral Symphony? Perhaps. Anyway, whatever it was, it was the perfect accompaniment to the view, quintessentially English, oh bugger, what was it called? Oh never mind.

His stomach rumbled, noisily. Patting it, he turned away from the splendour before him and, the musical mind-worm still wriggling inside his head, crept back into the tent to retrieve his portable stove. Within minutes, the air was filled with the rushing sound of burning camping gas, minutes later the aroma of fresh brewed coffee added to the ambience. As he took his first sip of the steaming liquid, he thought to himself I am in heaven…

***

The early morning mist had long since burned off by the time he had the tent packed away and strapped to the bottom of his rucksack. Giving the bag one last shrug into position, happy that everything was balanced and that nothing inside was digging into his back, he began walking, an oblong of flattened grass the only evidence he had been there at all.

His descent of the hill was via a thin track worn into the grass. A stile climbed over the dry stone wall that separated the hill from the road and he clambered over it gingerly, careful not to make any sudden movements at the top and possibly overbalance. It was a high wall, a fall from the top of it would do some damage. He negotiated the obstacle safely though and, after a quick check of the folded map which dangled from his belt wrapped in waterproof plastic, he turned to the left and began walking down the single track road.

It was a clear day and the sun shone from a cloudless sky. There was a chill in the air though, a proper autumnal feel to the day. His favourite time of year, always had been. Summer was too hot – and too busy with other people – for him to fully appreciate and enjoy his pastime of walking. Winter was dramatic, but too cold for camping, so it was the Autumn that he always chose to take his main holidays of the year, to head out into the countryside, to lose himself…

Today's destination was to be the (sleepy, or so he hoped) hamlet of Elder's End – a hike of some ten miles. As a treat to himself he would book into the local hostelry (he'd noted the PH symbol on the map next to one of the small cluster of buildings and hoped that they might do accommodation too) for the night, enjoy a few ales – around a roaring log fire – and a proper night's sleep in a bed. The thought of such luxury put a spring in his step and he strode onwards, invigorated.

A short detour from the road took him down to a gurgling stream that ran through a copse of trees and there he had lunch, a sandwich bought in a shop the day before and a cereal bar. Despite the chill in the air, midges swarmed above the water, their tiny bodies like motes of dust in the sunshine. A plopping noise distracted him and he saw a pattern of ripples moving outwards on the surface of the stream, the fish long gone, no doubt with a mouth full of midge. He took a swig of water from his bottle and sighed contentedly.

He lingered at the stream for longer than he should have and the sun was already low in the sky as he resumed his journey towards Elder's End. A few clouds had appeared but the chill was deeper and he was glad to be on the move again, generating his own heat.

Ironically, it was just as he was beginning to contemplate how quiet the road had been so far – no need to constantly stop and clamber up onto the verge to let vehicles past – when he heard the car coming towards him. The winding road meant he couldn't see too far ahead but the engine sounds suggested the car was moving at quite some speed. This was confirmed as the black Ford Focus hurtled past him without even slowing, the driver seemingly in so much of a hurry that he was unaware of his presence.

"Wanker!" he shouted at the disappearing car, adding the appropriate hand gesture. What's his hurry..? He dusted himself down, swishing away the dust thrown up by the car from his Berghaus jacket. No sooner had he stepped down from the verge back onto the road than he heard another vehicle approaching. Fuck sake…

This second vehicle was a VW camper van driven by a grey haired woman crouched intently behind the wheel. It was travelling a lot slower than the Focus and he saw a man, presumably the husband, sat up front alongside the woman, staring fixedly ahead. Again neither occupant of the van appeared aware of his presence.

This time he made it back onto the road and began walking again. Elder's End was just over a couple of miles away by his reckoning, he should be there in good time, an hour or so before it got dark, enough time to sample the delights of the local hostelry before retiring for the night…

The third vehicle was a pick-up truck. This was followed by a Renault Clio, a motorbike, a Fiesta – it was round about the twentieth vehicle that he stopped bothering to identify them. Where had they all come from? Where were they going? All day on his own and then this, this flurry – what was all that about?

It was an exodus, that was the word and the silence that followed it was profound. He hesitated for a while after the last vehicle had passed, checking to make sure that indeed it was the last. Satisfied this was the case, he began walking again. Maybe it's the residents of Elder's End, he mused, must have heard I was coming…

He passed by the squashed remains of a pheasant, one wing pointing upwards, feathers splayed to give the impression of a grasping hand. Fresh roadkill, a victim of the convoy that had just passed. He avoided looking at the bird's eyes, small black marbles that gazed lifelessly in bewilderment and quickened his pace.

***

The sinking feeling that had gripped him as he crested the hill overlooking Elder's End whereupon he had seen the hamlet in darkness, not a light to be seen inside or outside any of the buildings that huddled there intensified as he made his way past a row of houses towards the pub. Like the houses, it too stood in darkness. Images of supping a pint of ale in front of a roaring fire slowly melted away, along with those of lying down on a plush mattress and pulling the duvet over himself… He knocked anyway, on the large, black wooden door above which a sign proclaimed J Squires as the proprietor but wasn't at all surprised to receive no answer.

Fuck sake…

Slowly, he turned away from the door, slowly, dejection filled him. His rucksack suddenly felt a lot heavier, its straps dug painfully into his shoulders, the ache in the small of his back from carrying it had intensified. The exodus of vehicles that had passed him on his way here must have been the residents of Elder's End after all, there could be no other reason for the lack of any signs of life in the village. But where had they been going, and why in such a hurry?

Twilight had fallen, the sun having just disappeared behind the horizon, lending the world a grey cast. There was nothing for it, he would be spending another night under canvas – or nylon, if you were being precise – and instead of a pint of ale and some warming pub grub it would be instant coffee and sausages and beans from a tin. He shrugged his shoulders in a vain attempt to relieve some of the pressure on them and dejectedly headed back along the road towards the public footpath sign he'd seen on the way in. He'd have to pitch his tent somewhere out along the path, not too far along though, he certainly wasn't going to hump all this kit any further than he had to. A chill had descended, the crisp air he so enjoyed in the morning or to walk through during the day was less of a pleasure at this time of the evening. He soon reached the sign and unlatched the gate to gain access to the path that headed into some trees. He slammed the gate shut behind him with rather more force than was actually required and strode into the woods.

The trees still bore some leaves and the canopy reduced the light even further so he walked in darkness along the path that wound its way between massive trunks. Without thinking about it, his pace quickened until he was almost trotting through the trees, a tingling in the small of his back displacing the pain that had built up there. A man of his age scared of the dark? - how ridiculous. Instinct, he told himself, a primal fear of being in the woods in the dark developed by ancient ancestors, back when doing precisely that really was a risky business.

He stumbled and almost fell, arms cartwheeling wildly as he strove to regain his balance. He managed to do so, discovered that he was breathing heavily, that his heart was pounding in his chest.

Pull yourself together. Fuck sake…

He squinted into the gloom and felt a surge of relief as a gap in the darkness slowly came into view. Not much further till he was out of the woods. Already chastising himself for being such a coward, he shrugged the rucksack back into position and strode towards the exit from the copse. Within moments he exited the darkness of the trees and he sighed deeply as he stepped out into a field. Daft bugger.

After a few minutes exploring he decided the field was where he would pitch camp. At the far side of the field from the trees a small stream ran and it was near this that he began setting up the tent. It was almost as dark in the field now as it had been in the woods and he had to turn on his torch to allow enough light to see what he was doing. Even as he erected the tent he'd decided to forgo food for the night. It had been bad planning on his behalf, making an assumption about the pub. It would teach him a lesson to go hungry. His stomach rumbled, rubbing salt into his self-inflicted wounds.

Half an hour later, he was in his sleeping bag attempting to read the paperback novel he'd brought with him. He could see the words but none seemed to be sinking in, his sense of self-pity making it impossible to focus on anything other than how shitty he felt right then. Not even the sound of the stream nearby, usually soothing and soporific, could relax him. Sighing deeply, he tossed the book to the foot of the sleeping bag and flicked off the torch. Muttering under his breath, he snuggled into the bag, wrapping it tightly around himself.

Surprisingly, sleep came quickly.

***

He awoke to the sound of laughter, jolting awake suddenly. The sound came again, high-pitched and effervescent, more of a giggle…

"What the..?"

The laughter stopped, only to be replaced by the sounds of footsteps. Someone was outside the tent. Fully awake now, the surreal nature of the situation sunk home. Someone was outside the tent… someone was laughing outside the tent…

The footsteps stopped and the silence that followed it was even more disconcerting than the sound itself. He glanced at his watch, squinted in the darkness to make out the hands. Ten to three..? Whc on earth would be out and about at this time?

All at once he became aware of the sound of his heart beating, the thump-thump-thump filling the silence that enveloped him. Despite the cold of the night, a coldness that had seeped into the tent, he felt sweat prickle on his forehead.

Thump-thump-thump...

Slowly, he reached an arm out of the sleeping bag, winced at the rustling sound it made (like whoever's out there doesn't already know you're in here...) and groped around beside him for the torch. His hand found the cold plastic tube and he picked the torch up.

Okay. Now what?

He hesitated, indecision filled him. What exactly was he going to do? There had been no sounds from outside for a few minutes now and the thought that he may actually have just dreamt them in the first place occurred to him.

Another giggle came from outside the tent, shattering that particular notion and a fresh wave of horror swept over him as he realised that whoever was laughing outside was young – very young, a kid. Drunks messing about would have been bad enough but at least there would be a reason for that, a rationale... But a kid? What was a child doing out there in the dark at this time of night?

Thump-thump-thump-thump...

The giggling stopped (although the sound still echoed in his head) and once again the footsteps started, the pattern quicker this time – running, not walking – and getting louder. Whoever it was out there was running towards the tent and the realisation made him cry out, a shriek - more a squeak truth to tell - and drop the torch. Instinctively he covered his head with his hands, ducked down into the sleeping bag.

Something – someone – hit the tent at speed and he felt and heard the structure shake around him. He shrieked again but the sound was drowned out by the return of the giggling from outside. The laughter intensified – became manic – as his nocturnal intruder grabbed hold of the top of the pole at the head of the tent, the one alongside which he lay, and began to pull it backwards and forwards. The nylon of the tent rippled and stretched as the pole was pulled to and fro. The giggling intensified, so too his screams. The pole was let go and it twanged back into place.

Thump-thump-thump-thump...

His breathing was hoarse and laboured, sweat poured from his forehead, stinging his eyes. The side of the tent bulged in as hands were placed against it. Galvanised now by the adrenalin flooding his system he grabbed for the torch and turned it on, pointing the beam at the indentations in the side of the tent, saw the beam illuminate the impressions of two hands in the nylon, two small hands...

Those hands then began to beat a rhythm on the side of the tent, pummelling and slapping the nylon. More giggling accompanied the thumping (of his heart and the tent), the most terrifying sound he had ever heard. Tears sprang to his eyes. "Go away!" he shrieked, "fuck off away from here!"

The pounding increased in rhythm and intensity and he feared the tent would collapse in on itself, exposing him to the frenzied creature outside.

And then it stopped.

As if a switch had been thrown, the pummelling hands disappeared. Another short burst of giggles cut through the ensuing silence and then he heard footsteps running away from the tent.

He couldn't move. As hard as he tried, he was unable even to wiggle a finger. He felt locked in place, his breath came in short, sharp bursts. A stinging in his eyes informed him that he hadn't even blinked for some time so he did and this conscious effort somehow began to free him from his rigor.

What the hell was that? As some form of normality returned to his body, the extreme abnormality of what he'd just seen and heard struck him like a hammer blow.

What was a kid doing out here at this time of night? Where were the parents? Even as he asked himself the second question an answer of sorts popped into his head. Skipped town in the convoy...

That made sense – and yet made no sense at all. He began to shake, not only from the cold but he slipped back into the sleeping bag anyway. The thought that he should go out and investigate crossed his mind but was quickly dismissed. The incident was over, he tried to convince himself, there would be no good at all in him stumbling around in the dark looking for something that wasn't even there.

Very convincing argument...
Convincing enough. He shuffled deeper into the sleeping bag and pulled the top of it over his head, not in any way acting like a frightened little boy hiding under the covers. He listened, and listened for the sounds of more activity outside the tent but none came and eventually he fell into a deep sleep.

***

Despite his lack of food the previous night, the insistent pressure in his bladder was the same as it always was when he awoke in the twilight of the new day. He hurriedly extricated himself from the sleeping bag and, dressing quickly, crawled out of the tent. The light was dim but enough to allow him a view of his surroundings which had been denied him last night when he'd pitched camp in darkness.

The wood he'd cut through, and which had spooked him at the time – although not as much as later events had – were forty yards or so behind him, providing a pretty effective barrier between the field and Elder's End. The stream ran directly alongside where he'd pitched the tent, an eroded bankside giving steep access to it. On the other side of the stream lay more woods. Resisting the urging from his bladder, he made a circuit of the tent, looking for evidence of last night's incursion. He found none, no footprints in the dew that covered the grass apart from his own. A dream then? Perhaps – but an incredibly vivid one if it was. He wasn't convinced.

He could hold back the flow no longer though and quickly scuttled down to the edge of the stream. Happy that the bank-side would hide him from anyone passing by, he unzipped and began to piss. Not that there were likely to be any passers-by, he guessed that any early morning dog walkers would have been part of the exodus too.

It was as he turned to make his way back up to the tent that something caught his eye on the far bank of the river. Something hanging from a branch of one of the trees. He moved closer to the stream's edge to get a better look. Small, brown and furry – Oh shit! It's a dead animal! – but no, as he squinted, he saw that it wasn't an animal at all, well- not a real one anyway – what hung suspended from the tree was a teddy bear. How bizarre... And there, beyond the dangling bear, something else. He stepped forward, felt the water wash over his boot and immediately stepped back. It was a toy train, he was sure of it.

Intrigued, he searched for a crossing point in the stream and soon came to one, a line of stones providing a natural ford. He quickly stepped over the slippery surfaces, arms spread wide to aid balance, safely reaching the other side of the stream. He walked into the trees ahead of him, passed by the teddy bear – threadbare and worn, one eye missing – and confirmed that the second object he'd seen was indeed a toy train, wooden and painted in garish colours. Both toys had been hung from the branches with thick twine. More toys were now visible, all hanging from branches like strange fruit, here a doll, there a skittle, over there a football (in a net to allow hanging) on the tree behind an Action Man.

The sight was utterly bizarre and yet somehow moving. What could be the purpose of it? Was it some strange ritual enacted by the residents of Elder's End (something he could readily believe given yesterday's events) or was it some kind of memorial, some kind of shrine?

The last idea caused him to shiver but somehow it felt right, felt appropriate. Whatever the explanation, he was beginning to feel a little exposed here, a little nervous. In light of what had happened in the middle of the night – something he now knew had definitely not been a dream – this strange place had suddenly taken on a more sinister aspect.

He turned to head back to the tent, noticing as he did that one of the toys had fallen from its tree to the ground beneath. A doll, he saw, quite a large one – which may explain why it had fallen. It lay on its back, its feet towards him, arms spread out to either side. He was momentarily halted in his tracks by the sight, it looked so realistic.

That's because…

Oh shit, no, surely not..? The thought made him nauseous and he had to take deep breaths to prevent himself from being sick. Not wanting to, but knowing he must, he began to walk towards the prone figure. Please, please, please let me be wrong.

The doll moved. A slight shuffle that disturbed the leaves around it but enough to stop him in his tracks. Oh my God, she's alive! The doll moved again, slowly raising itself to its feet. Not a doll then, but surely not a little girl either, or no normal little girl at least for it was as if the figure levitated to a standing position, rocking forward on its heels, driven forwards and upwards by some unseen force, its arms remaining outstretched at its sides offering no assistance to the movement.

"Oh no..." he croaked, felt the rigidity of fear from last night overwhelm him again.

The girl now stood upright, her head bowed. Slowly she raised that head to look at him though whether she could see anything through those eyes of milky whiteness was not certain. She giggled, a sound so horribly familiar to him and it cut through his rigidity, turned his legs to jelly and he fell, unsupported to the ground.

The girl raised her arms towards him, offered dirty hands to him, the dirt ingrained beneath the fingernails. "Will you play with us?" She asked.

He screamed as the thing began to walk towards him. A noise came from behind him, more rustling in the carpet of leaves that covered the floor of the wood. He didn't need to turn and see what was making the noise, he already knew.

"Will you play with us?"

The End.

Case #63284

Anthony Watson

I run a small press myself, along with Ross Warren called Dark Minds and have so far published two anthologies of dark fiction. I've had some success with being published in the small press and will have a story, Interstice, in next year's Christmas ghost story annual from Spectral Press. Some of my other stories can be accessed at castingrunes.co.uk and I have a review blog, Dark Musings, at anthony-watson.blogspot.co.uk

CLAYTON HILL SANITARIUM

CLAYTON HILL SANITARIUM
Curiosity
Anthony Camarillo
Physician: Dr. Peterson
8268-WCT29
74

"Dude, Kotah, are you gonna pass that or am I gonna have to wait until you wake up tomorrow?"

It was either Steven's voice or the burning sensation on my thigh that snapped me out of my stoned stupor, but I couldn't be sure; the roaming light in the distance held my attention at that moment. From our position, seated atop the roof of my parents' two-story home, I could see the dark outlining of what appeared to be a car traveling west on Los Lobos Street, toward my own street, Long Avenue. A light of some sort glared from the passenger window, blanketing homes with a pale brightness as it made its way towards the intersection.

"Wake up, man! Your shorts are catching fire!"

"Huh?"

Not until I looked down did I notice that Steven was right, to an extent. My shorts were on fire but it wasn't anything to be alarmed at. A piece of the pot that was lit inside the bowl of the pipe must have popped out and, at that moment, was burning its way through my khaki shorts. I cursed the blazing escape artist, swept it off my lap with a quick hand and then handed the pipe back to Steven.

Problem solved. That was, until the approaching car came into focus and I realized exactly what it was.

The police cruiser reached Long Avenue and came to a complete halt at the stop sign. Sure, there was nothing in the law that said I couldn't sit on my own roof in the middle of the night, but smoking illegal marijuana on my roof was another thing. While my intoxicated mind worked its way to a sensible route of action, the searchlight on the side of the cruiser worked its way to our lofty hiding spot.

"Shit!"

Shit was right, a whole lot of shit and a goddamn pile of the stuff, if you'd like. That's exactly what we were about to be in if Steven or myself didn't think of something fast.

The searchlight began to creep across the driveway like a makeshift sun, slowly illuminating every inch of the yard and as it rose, so did the speed of my heartbeats.

Thump.

"Dude, toss the fucking thing!" Steven spoke quiet and sharply, slowly retreating up the roof and towards the backyard. I couldn't remember Steven giving Tiger Weeds back to me but nevertheless, it was in my hand.

"I'm not getting caught with that," I heard him say as he scurried over to the opposite side of the roof.

Thump.Thump.

Without giving myself a second more to come up with a plan, I turned to my left and lightly, under-hand tossed the pipe into the bushes on my neighbor's side of the fence. I let it sail to the ground twenty feet below, tensing up as I anticipated the sound of shattering glass.

Thump.Thump.Thump.

As Tiger Weeds submerged itself into the foliage of Mr. Crespin's garden, I could hear Steven landing in the backyard behind my house.

"Kotah, get your ass back here!" The shakiness in his voice was enough to show me I wasn't the only one who thought I would be riding in the back of a cop car that night.

Thump.Thump.Thump.Thump.

The black and white cruiser was finally at a complete stop in the gutter in front of my house and the spotlight had managed to reach the tiles of the roof, no more than six feet below me. I didn't have much time left to think about it so I turned back towards the side of the house that sat between Mr. Crespin's yard and our own and took a leap of faith. And when I say leap of faith, I don't mean it in the figurative sense; I took a deep breath, prayed that I wouldn't break my ankle and jumped off the fucking roof.

***

After about five minutes that felt closer to five hours, I raised my cheek off the cool grass and turned my head in the direction of the street. No cruiser left to see. It must have crept away as quietly as it had come, I thought to myself as I picked myself up from the ground.

"Is he gone?" Steven whispered from the other side of the fence that led into my backyard, his voice with the amount of courage in it that a child has when he knows he just might be escaping an encounter with the belt. Just maybe.

"Yeah, but so is Tiger Weeds," I replied back into the shadows.

"Did it break?" Steven's voice was blanketed in a thin layer of relief. The pipe was the least of his worries. What we were both thankful for was the fact that we were still free and undetected.

"Maybe," I started but then quickly corrected myself, "Well, more than likely, yeah. I didn't hear it break but it wasn't made out of rubber. I'm sure it's in pieces at the bottom of those bushes."

I motioned towards the bushes in my neighbor's yard. Amidst the greenery that stood about the same height as myself, a twinkle caught my eye as I turned back to Steven. With a quick double take I discovered that Tiger Weeds was still in one piece and also within reach.

"Maybe it is made out of rubber after all," Steven mumbled as his eyes fell on the bushes. It was enough to melt away any lasting anxiety and for the next few moments, Steven and I stood in the dark, laughing away like anyone stoned in their front yard at two in the morning would do.

Once the thoughts of the police cruiser evaporated into the sky like spilt beer on a summer afternoon, we decided that there were still hours left in the night, not to mention pot still left in the plastic, green baggy tucked away in Steven's shirt pocket. We agreed that the roof wasn't a safe place to smoke anymore, or at least for tonight, but that didn't mean we couldn't find a safer place to hide away and ease our minds.

At about a quarter past two, Steven and I made our way up Long Avenue, heading south towards Vision Canyon Road. Long Avenue could be a creepy street at night. With no light to illuminate the street besides two lampposts at either end of the street, the moon and the slight glow that emanated from television-lit windows, the middle of the street was a very dark place. It was the sort of road where you expected to see a tumbleweed roll across, followed by a sharp wind and the howl of a distant coyote. Luckily though, with the cop gone, we wouldn't have to take part in any showdowns tonight.

"Who lives there?" Steven asked, tilting his head to the home on our left. The house he was motioning towards was one of the only homes on the block of which I didn't know the residents. For the most part, Estate Hills was a small town with a tightly knit community, but somehow, people could still slip through the cracks of public notice. The single-story, ranch-style home that Steven was observing must have belonged to people of that sort.

"No idea. Now that I think about it, I've never noticed cars

parked in front of it either," I replied.
"Well, nothing's changed tonight."
I nodded my head, staring at the wide, rectangular windows that faced the street like dead, vacant eyes. As I did, an indiscernible dread washed over me like a bucket of cold water.
"Yeah, let's find a different spot though. I don't know who lives there," I told him.
"Well, you said you never see cars parked in front right? Maybe nobody lives here," Steven continued, "I mean, by the looks of the yard, it looks pretty damn deserted to me."
He was right, at least in the sense that it looked deserted. The weeds were slowly turning the yard into their own stomping ground and the grass (what was left of it, at least) needed to be watered just as badly as the home's white exterior could use a fresh coat of paint. The home was a mess, without a welcoming feature in sight, and the wrought iron bars that guarded the windows only helped to increase its repellant nature. If anyone did live there, public appearance was not very high on their list of priorities.
"Yeah, but still, I don't know for sure and I don't feel like waiting to find out."
"Don't be such a little girl about it," Steven rebutted. He wasn't a reckless person when it came down to it but he did have a rebellious streak in him and the glint in his eye was enough to tell me that streak just shot across his mind like a shooting star.
"You're the one who's rolling your eyes like a girl," I shot back, "All I'm saying is that we barely dodged the cops earlier and I'm not trying to test my luck a second time."
Steven sighed and looked back to the house. His stubbornness was overriding his sensibility and I knew it was only a matter of time until he took it upon himself to make himself at home in the front yard. Slowly but surely, he made his way into the yard and it only took me seconds to make up my mind to follow him. Irrational ideas have an infectious air about them.
Something about the house just wasn't right and I could feel it with every step I took in its direction. It was like being watched but still, those windows kept on drawing us in like moths to a flame. Whether I liked it or not, I was caught in a web of curiosity and I only became more entangled the closer I got.
"Looks like we're wrong bud. There's a light on in there." Steven was on the lawn in front of the long, rectangular window. I couldn't

see what he was looking in at; his shape was blocking my sight.

"Do you see anyone in there?"

"No. But I guess people do live here; there's a TV on," he replied in a preoccupied tone. At that moment I decided to join him in his voyeuristic search but that wave of unpleasantness washed over me again and froze me mid-step.

"Well, there you have it man. People do live here. Now, let's get the fuck out of here before we get charged with marijuana possession and trespassing."

I knew Steven heard me but apparently it didn't register; he stood still as the trees along the side of the house.

"Steven, are you still stoned or what? Let's leave."

Still no response.

I wanted to leave him there, staring stupidly into the glass, but I just couldn't find it in myself to do it; I might not see him again. Sure, I was uncomfortable but a bad friend was something I couldn't be. Steven could be hardheaded sometimes but all in all, I thought he was a good guy.

I decided to make my way closer when he put a hand up to subdue me.

"Don't come closer."

"What?"

"I said not to come any closer," Steven repeated, this time with more authority in his voice.

"Stev—"

"—Shut up, man! I'm trying to listen!"

Listen? I wondered what he could've possibly been listening for.

"How could it—How could anyone know..."

"What does who know?"

"I don't like this house, man. You're right, let's get the fuck out of here," he spoke again. The shakiness in his voice sent a chill down my spine like nothing else could in the middle of August. I admitted to myself that I didn't feel confident standing in that strange yard, staring ahead at an even stranger house, but the sound in his voice was unmistakable. He was scared shitless.

"What's in there?"

"Nothing."

"Nothing? Bullshit. You don't look like you just saw nothing. What did you see?"

Steven stayed silent. At that moment I wanted nothing more than to walk up to the windowpane, cup my hands around my eyes and peer into the glass, but that uneasy feeling persisted. Intuition was warning enough; I knew that I wasn't going to like whatever it was that my imagination wanted to behold. If there was ever a time that I wanted to leave my problems behind in a cloud of smoke, it was then.

"Kotah, I'm going home now. I think you should too."

"Are you serious?"

"Yeah, man. I don't really feel like smoking after all. I don't really feel like doing anything right now, actually. I'm gunna go home and get some rest," without another word, Steven walked past me and began heading toward his home on Los Lobos Street like a man in a trance.

"You better tell me what the hell you're tripping out about tomorrow!" I called back to him but the words sailed over his head like dust.

I figured that whatever it was that Steven saw was important enough to see that very moment. I gravitated closer to the window. My muscles tensed and I held my breath as I allowed myself to see what I had been warned against.

Unfortunately, I saw nothing. Well, not in the literal sense of things, but nothing of major importance. As I put my forehead against the glass, I peered into a poorly lit, rectangular room. The room was dark except for a single bulb that hung from the center of the ceiling on a long, brown chord. Besides an old television (that looked as if the last time it was considered "high-tech" was sometime around the mid 1970's) and the wooden stepstool it rested upon, the room was devoid of any furniture. The television was a pale blue hue with a blank, convex screen, along with small, black knobs running alongside the screen that most likely took the place of its nonexistent remote control.

Despite the fact that I hadn't yet noticed that the room had no visible door to enter or exit through, the room didn't seem too out of the ordinary. It was an empty room with one light and one broken television. I was immediately angry at my childish fears and even madder at Steven for acting so weird and then leaving without explanation.

"He was probably bullshitting me," I said aloud to myself. Whether I actually thought this or just told it to myself as reassurance, I couldn't be sure. But the fact that he lost all interest in being out and simply wanted to go home to sleep was completely against his nature and that's what nagged at me. Steven looked genuinely. I no longer wanted to stand outside that window; I felt that I had outstayed my welcome.

Once I composed myself, I turned away and began walking back towards my house. When I reached the street, I turned back to the house and gave it one more look. The pale light that had emanated from the glass was no longer. Somehow, the light bulb was no longer lit.

***

Days had passed since the night I spent with Steven outside of the house up the street and I still hadn't managed to interpret the puzzle inside my head. Steven hadn't returned any of my calls and none of his three roommates had seen him since that night. They suggested that he probably went to a girl's house that night after he left from my house but something in me told me that just couldn't be the case.

I figured I would eventually see him on a shift since we worked at the same record store but he had even failed to make it to work. It took two no-call-no-show's until our manager began to worry as well and decided to try to get in touch with him but even he was greeted with Steven's answering machine, time after time. I later visited his parents' home in Blaggston to see if they had heard from him or at least knew where he was but they were even less informed than myself. What I thought at first to be a joke on his part slowly turned into a matter of a missing person. Unfortunately, that was just the tip of the iceberg.

Although my main concern was for my friend's well being, I became increasingly entranced with the mystery that hung like a sinister cloud over the neighboring house up the street. I began changing the routes I took to and from school, as well as work, so that I would get a chance to pass by the house in the hopes that I would catch a glimpse of the inhabitants, but still I saw nothing. That was, until a full week had passed.

The more often I passed in front of the house, I began to realize that the light would go on whenever I would drive pass it. It gave me the sense that perhaps there was some sort of motion-censor that activated the light whenever I would pass in front of it but the idea was weakly supported. I mean, who puts a motion-censor light inside their home? It was as if the house was trying to get my attention, giving me the light bulb as bait whenever I would be within sight of it. The idea was crazy, but so was the fact that my best friend had gone missing.

Once Steven's absence from society became apparent to the rest of his peers, I realized that it was finally time to get the authorities involved. I mean, for all I knew, he could have been kidnapped on his way home that night. Being twenty-two doesn't exclude a person from being a potential kidnapping victim, unfortunately.

As the number of days increased since I had last seen Steven, so did the number of missing-person fliers. Even people who didn't like him or know him began to talk about his disappearance until it became somewhat of a local phenomenon. Everyone began to wonder where the guy was until it got to the point where I could have sworn he had last been seen wearing a red and white striped sweater with a red beanie, except "Where's Steven?" was not my idea of a fun game. I didn't want to think of the word dead but it kept crawling back like a stray cat.

He's not dead, he can't be dead.

But why couldn't he be? People don't go missing, skip their shifts, avoid their friends and family, and then come home like it hadn't happened at all. Things like that don't happen; that was just not the way of the world and I knew it.

That's the pessimist in you, Kotah.

Maybe, but I was doing my best to prepare for the worst, in case that little, negative bastard on my shoulder was right.

Then, just when I began to think the situation was as bad and as hopeless as it was going to get, things got a lot worse.

My phone began to ring in the middle of the night, easing me out of my dead sleep and back to the land of the conscious. As my eyes did their best to adjust to the black blanket of darkness that enveloped my room, my hand fumbled across books and a few pens that laid askew on my nightstand until it finally reached its target. I pressed the green answer button (more out of muscle memory rather than conscious decision making) and set the phone against my ear.

"Yeah?"

"Wake up, Kotah."

My heart sunk in my chest. Not like how the Titanic did, slowly and with enough time for Leo and Kate to doggy-paddle around in the water for a bit. No, my heart sunk like an anchor, heavy and swift.

"Who—Who's this?" But I didn't have to ask; I already knew the answer. I knew that voice like I knew my own.

It was Steven on the other end of the line.

***

"Have you watched TV lately, Kotah?"

"TV? What?"

"Yeah, you know, the box with the pictures that come on the screen? I know you know what I'm talking about."

My friend was missing for over two weeks and all he had bothered to call me for was to ask if I had been keeping up with television shows like It's Always Sunny In Philadelphia.

"Yes I know what you're talking about," I replied, doing my best to remain patient with him, "You woke me up. I'm still out of it. Where the hell are you Steven?"

"You didn't answer my question. Did you watch TV lately? Have you even turned it on since the night we left that house? Have you passed by any televisions at all since then?"

That house, I knew it was something about that house. When I began to think harder, I remembered him saying something about the TV being on when he looked through the window.

But was it on when you looked, Kotah? It wasn't, huh?

"What did you see in that window, Steven? What happened to you? I'm worried about you, man. We're all worried about you. Just come home."

Silence.

I waited a long time until I almost thought he had hung up until he began talking again.

"Something is wrong with that house, Kotah. It's like those windows draw you in and then the TV looks inside you, inside your soul. It saw who I was, it saw past all the bullshit and it showed me who I was, the part of me that I've always tried to hide."

It was my turn to be silent.

"When I looked inside, I saw a TV and in moments it showed me every single thing I had ever done wrong. I'm a horrible person,

Kotah. I should have never looked into that fucking house—but I was curious!"

I lurched away from my phone as he spat the last words out. It seemed more like he was trying to convince himself, rather than me.

"You remember that German guy we learned about in class? What was his name?" he pondered to himself and at that moment it felt as if I wasn't listening to my friend speak anymore, but instead, some sort of stranger.

"Nietzsche. That was his name. He summed it up perfectly. He said, 'When you look into the abyss, the abyss also looks into you.' That's what I did. I looked where I shouldn't have looked and just because I was curious," he said the word quickly as if the taste would be too much for him if he didn't spit it out fast enough.

"I was curious, so the house showed me how dark my heart is."

"Steven, you're a good guy. I don't know what the fuck you're talking about. Stop talking crazy and please just go home. At least call your parents and tell them you're okay."

I said the words but I knew they lacked conviction. Steven was beginning to scare me with every word he spoke. As I sat up in bed, waiting for his response, the clouds shifted in the sky, allowing for a ray of moonlight to pass through the shutters. A pale, ghastly glow fell upon my television screen and I could see my face reflected in it. I shivered a bit although the room wasn't cold.

"Do you remember that party we threw at my house for my twenty-first birthday? That night when a bunch of the sorority girls from Cal State Fullerton came?"

"Yes," I didn't quite remember the specifics of the party but I dimly recalled what he was talking about.

"I raped one of those girls."

He said it with ease but the disgust in his voice was there, the way a lampshade hid the bulb beneath. It was dim, but I could feel its presence.

"You—Come on… You woul—"

"Oh, but I did. She passed out on the floor of my room because she had too much to drink. I was drunk too but I knew what I was doing. I could have just left her or called for her friends… but no. Oh God…oh God, oh God, I'm a fucking animal!"

Stay calm, Kotah.

"Steven… Whether that's true or not, you can't run away from the past. Just come home and we can figure this thing out together," I didn't like the begging sound of my voice but I knew there was no other way, "Please, Steven. Please."

"No, I already know I'm not coming home. I've already made up my mind on that but I called you to warn you. We all have our skeletons and I'm sure you have yours too, so if you're smart, you'll listen. Don't look into that house and if you already have, don't turn on your TV. It'll show you your dark side and it'll worm its way inside you. It's a fucking parasite, Kotah. It'll eat you."

The call ended. I called his name into the receiver while I sat in the dark but I knew it was hopeless. Steven was gone. I began to dial the number to his parents' home but then I stopped and put the phone back. When I awoke the next morning, my television was on but there was only static across the screen.

***

From The Alley Catalog, September 3rd, 2012

ESTATE HILLS RESIDENT COMMITS SUICIDE IN LOCAL MOTEL

Broken Neck and Television Greet House Keeping

A member of the house keeping staff found the body of twenty-two-year-old Steven A. Rodriguez, a resident of Estate Hills, as well as an alumnus from the California State University of Los Angeles, Monday morning in a local Motel 6. "There wasn't a 'Do Not Disturb' sign on the door and when I knocked, nobody answered so I figured it would be okay to go inside and change the sheets," Mercedes, the housekeeper, told authorities. Rodriguez had managed to construct a makeshift noose out of USB-cables and tied them to the ceiling fan, effectively hanging himself. "I screamed when I saw him dangling from up there," Mercedes said, doing her very best to hold back her tears, "He looked so young." Besides a note that was left on top of the shattered television that read, "DO NOT LOOK AT THE TV. CURIOSITY KILLED THIS CAT," the room appeared to be void of any personal possessions. Rodriguez was originally reported missing by his family on August 20th and police plan to investigate this matter further. "My son knew the boy," said David Richardson, the Estate Hills police chief, "There wasn't a harmful bone in his body. Someone else had to have been at the bottom of this and we won't rest until we find out who that someone is."

The End.

Case #27662

Anthony Camarillo

My name is Anthony Camarillo and I was born in Anaheim Hills, California in 1992. I've been writing short fiction off and on since 2001 but decided to dive head first into the horror genre in 2010. I currently attend the California State University of Fullerton as a third year English major and member of the Pi Kappa Alpha fraternity, as well as working part-time at In-N-Out Burger. My hobbies consist of weight lifting, attending local hardcore and metal shows, watching horror and comedy films, as well as maintaining my urban-wear clothing company called Nasty Attire. The works of Stephen King, Dan Simmons, Joe Hill and J.K. Rowling are large influences on my own work, as well as bands such as Circa Survive, Title Fight, The Plot In You and Letlive.

CLAYTON HILL SANITARIUM

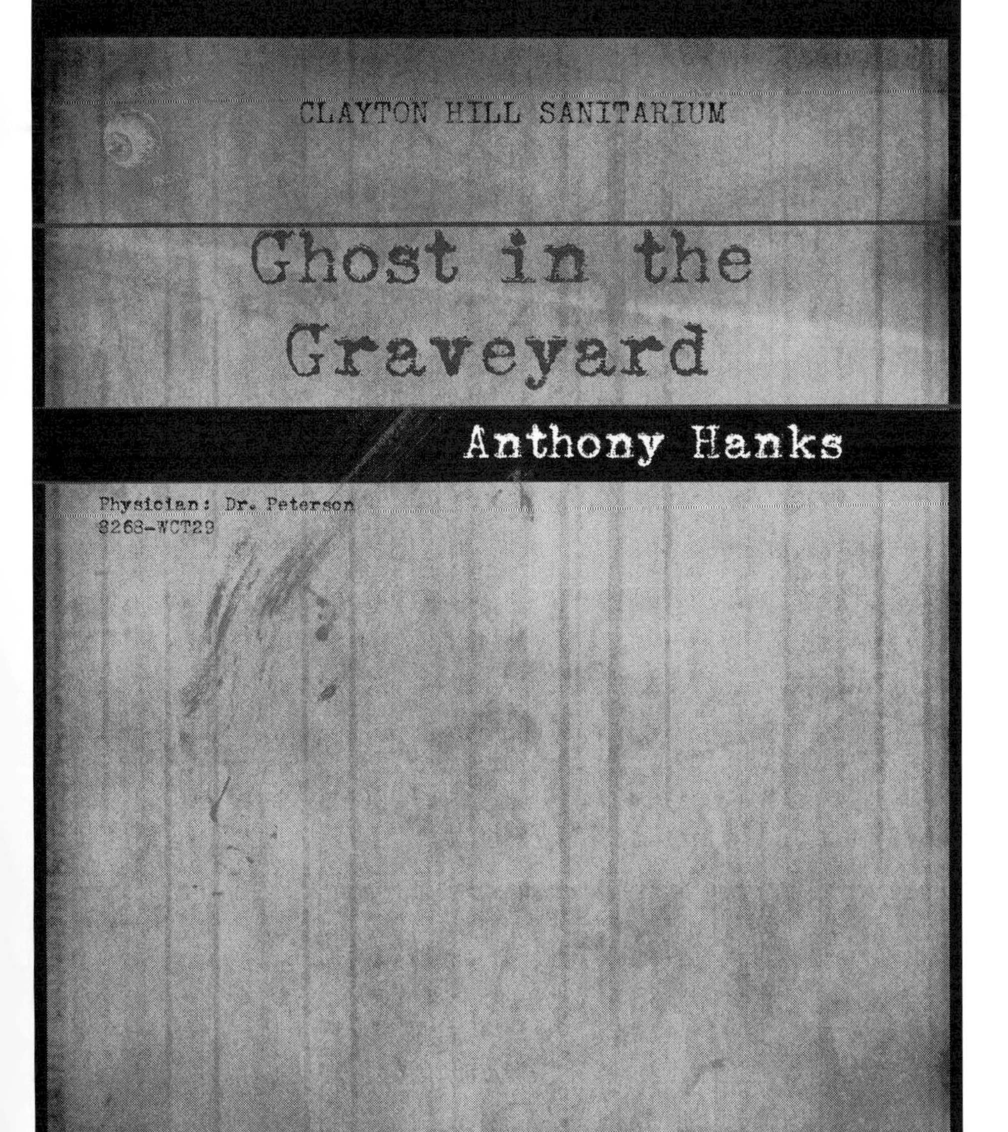

CLAYTON HILL SANITARIUM
Ghost in the Graveyard
Anthony Hanks
Physician: Dr. Peterson
8268-WCT29
86

I was twelve years old when my first friend died. I only wish he'd been the last. I would lose six more friends in as many years following that summer, but C.J. was the first. And the circumstances surrounding his death may have been the strangest.

Looking back it's actually amazing that we were friends at all. Our first couple of encounters were less than pleasant. I was a bit of a spoiled shit and came from money, at least by Conscience, Illinois standards. I'm not proud of it, but as a younger child I picked on kids less fortunate than myself and C.J. was certainly no exception. I don't remember how I'd picked on him (in those days it was probably a combination of name calling and rock throwing), but I do remember that he paid me back in spades by pissing in a squirt gun and giving me a face-full via bicycle drive-by.

That was when we were eight.

As fate would have it, C.J. and I wound up on the same little league team the following summer and he turned out to be every bit as good a short-stop as I was a second baseman. So, wounds healed, and two boys bonded over the Great American Pastime.

And nobody got pissed on.

Thankfully for me, the older I got, the more accepting I became of kids my age, regardless of their financial status. By the summer of my 12th birthday C.J. was one of about seven or eight of us kids that palled around together pretty regularly. The rest of our proverbial "Little Rascals" were as follows:

Clint. The typical country boy destined to inherit the family farm.

Amy. Guaranteed to do great things, just not guaranteed to leave Conscience, IL.

Wes and Wendy. The twins. They would die five and six years later, respectively.

Edie. Lovely Edie. I'd lose my virginity to her five years later, one week before the aforementioned Wes would try to beat a train across the railroad tracks and lose.

Becca. Short for Rebeca. Equally as lovely as Edie with curly, platinum blond hair. She would die in another seven years, after opening a bottle of vodka and later that evening, the arteries in both her wrists.

Me. Devilishly handsome, even at that young age, and most importantly, still alive, but probably only because I got out of that town before it could sink its teeth into me fully.

C.J. I've already told you about him. Piss shooter, salty shortstop, and dead at the age of twelve.

Now you know the players, so let's get back to this little campfire tale (if anyone actually tells stories around campfires anymore.) I regret to inform you that C.J.'s death was nothing as extravagant as a werewolf attack. Nothing as stylish as a Freddy Krueger-like child murder.

C.J. drowned. Plain and simple. He jumped off a train trestle forty feet above the Cahokia River and didn't surface again for 3 miles, where he washed up on a sandbar downriver. Funny thing, this trestle was only 300 yards from where Wes Klein (one of the twins), and his 1979 Chevy Monte Carlo were cut in half five years later by a Union Pacific coal train.

As I said, nothing unusual about a drowning. Sadly, they happen every day (I don't know if that's true, but with all the people in the world it probably is, right?)

The strange and unusual part of this story happened two weeks before C.J.'s death at Becca's birthday party. None of us recognized the significance of the event until after C.J. was dead and buried. To my knowledge none of us have mentioned it again until now.

Becca's birthday party was pretty typical by normal standards. The eight of us--Clint, Amy, the Twins, Edie, Becca, C.J. and me--got together at Becca's house and for the first part of the evening we played by the rules. Becca opened her presents, blew out her candles, and as far as her parents were concerned, the craziest thing we did that night was watch Child's Play and try to scare the shit out of each other. However, this was a special night. Some of us were allowed, and some of us flat lied, but all of us were attending our first co-ed sleepover. Once Becca's parents went to bed we all moved on to a particularly steamy round of spin-the-bottle.

I kissed a girl for the first time that night (not counting my mother or sister).

After a couple of hours of kissing, slobbering, and awkward groping we'd all grown tired of exploring each other's tonsils with our tongues so we were looking for something new to do that would occupy our time. Sex was still something we only joked about at that time and most of us were years away from that being a logical option. That's when Becca, the birthday girl herself, spoke up and asked if any of us wanted to play "Ghost in the Graveyard."

None of us did.

Ghost in the Graveyard was something you played in Elementary school. It was not something you did as an adventurous 7th grader. After giving Becca a hard time about suggesting such a lame activity she quickly hushed our group by asking us when we last played the game in an actual graveyard.

We instantly knew what she was getting at.

There were three cemeteries in Conscience (which seems excessive looking back, considering the town only had 1,400 people in it), and Becca lived directly across the street from the oldest, spookiest one in town. All of a sudden, Ghost in the Graveyard started to seem a lot less lame.

Trespassing in a graveyard at night has a spot on every Midwestern child's list of "must do" activities, right between toilet-papering the Phys Ed teacher's house and skinny dipping in one of the display pools at the local pool and spa distribution center. Becca's 13th birthday party suddenly provided our gang the opportunity to check off this particular rite of passage. And so, with a rekindled excitement for what we all essentially considered a kid's game, we agreed that we should play.

At this point I feel obligated to pause the story of C.J.'s death so that I can quickly explain the rules and gameplay for Ghost in the Graveyard. If you grew up in the Midwest playing this delightfully macabre version of tag on summer nights feel free to skip ahead. However, if you need a refresher, or if by some chance you've never hear of Ghost in the Graveyard, read on.

The game is essentially a combination of "tag" and "hide-and-go-seek." First off, a home base is established--usually a tree or something like that. Next, someone is chosen to be "the ghost." The ghost runs off to hide somewhere in the yard and everyone else stays at home base and counts to fifty. After that, the other players go out and attempt to find the ghost. If someone spots the ghost they shout "GHOST IN THE GRAVEYARD!" and everyone makes a break back towards home base while "the ghost" chases them. Anyone that's tagged also becomes a ghost for the next round. This goes on until only one person is left. Now, if the ghost isn't discovered immediately he has two options. First off, he can sneak around stealthily and avoid discovery, but eventually he'll need to move on to option two, which is to jump out of hiding and scare the others, and then attempt to tag as many people as he can before they can run back to Home Base.

Again, the game was fun in grade school, but I'll admit now, playing in an actual graveyard, at any age, is downright creepy.
With a mutual sharing of the uneasiness, we all headed across the street and hopped the gates of Antioch Cemetery.
As per the rules we established a home base by designating the flag pole at the front of the grounds. There wasn't a light on the flag, which I'm pretty sure is illegal, or at the very least disrespectful or something. I only mention it so that you understand that the cemetery was pitch black, with nothing but a sliver of moon to help us avoid shattered ankles as we ran around, or worse, an involuntary braining on a headstone.
I don't remember who the first few of us were that were selected as ghosts, but I do remember that for the initial 45 minutes or so none of us ventured too far away from that flag pole when it was our turn to hide. However, as the night wore on, we all slowly started migrating further and further away, until we had almost reached the far corners of the graveyard.
Then it was C.J.'s turn to be the ghost.
He ran off to hide and the rest of us stayed at the flagpole and started counting. When his time was up we all branched out and started exploring the rows of headstones and mausoleums. After about ten minutes I can remember being aware that nobody had made it that long without being found so I assumed that C.J. was probably on the move and keeping an eye on us from the shadow of some crypt. I distinctly remember getting chills at that point, at the thought of being stalked by someone in a graveyard, even if I did know exactly who it was that was doing the stalking, and the worst thing he could have done was spray me in the face with a little piss. But it could have just as easily been a vampire, and our little town had a legend about one of those, too. So with a fresh case of the creeps I pushed further into the dark cemetery.
I came upon a giant, twisted oak tree that looked like it could reach out and grab me and gobble me up. I knew this marked about the halfway point into the cemetery. I could hear the tail end of someone whispering "where the fuck is he?" about forty yards to my right, but I wasn't sure who exactly said it. It could have been any one of us because most of the guys' voices hadn't changed, so we all sounded the same, and at twelve it was cool to use "fuck" in every other sentence. Before I could give it another moment's thought, a giant werewolf jumped out from the other side of the

tree, his fangs dripping with blood. I fell backwards and screamed.
When I looked up I saw that the werewolf was actually Edie, who was laughing her ass off.
"Jesus Edie!" I said, somewhere between a whisper and a shout. "You scared the shit out of me."
"Yeah, but you're so cute when you're scared." Edie stuck her hand out and helped me up, and once my pulse rate got back to normal (and she stopped giggling), we continued further into the graveyard.
That's when Becca started to scream.
I was convinced that it really WAS a werewolf this time, and he was tearing her to pieces, but when she began to scream again I could make out discernible words.
"GHOST IN THE GRAVEYARD! GHOST IN THE GRAVEYARD!"
That was our queue to run like hell. Edie and I took off for the flag pole, confident that we were pretty safe because Becca had screamed from the far back right corner of the graveyard, and we'd gotten an easy thirty yard head start. Edie ran cross-country in Junior High, so I'm embarrassed to say that she quickly began to out distance me. I could see in my peripheral that everyone else had heard Becca's scream as well and they were hurdling headstones to make it back to home base. I pushed on, focusing a little too much on Edie's toned ass in her cutoff jean shorts, so I didn't notice at first when C.J. jumped out from behind a big crypt and grabbed her, just twenty yards shy of the flag pole.
Unlike Becca, Edie's scream really was full of terror. C.J. wrapped his arms around her, and because I was utterly shocked that he'd managed to somehow, almost impossibly, pull in front of us, my brain couldn't shut my feet down in time and I plowed into them both at full speed. The three of us went down hard, blessedly shy of a headstone, with Edie sandwiched between C.J. and me like a gothic ménage a trois. Once we all got our breath back we managed to stand up just as the rest of the crew came over to see what all the commotion was about. Edie had bit her tongue when we went down and she'd start to spit blood and cry. C.J. and I turned back to each other and simultaneously shouted, "WHAT THE FUCK?!?"
This was followed by an intense shoving match--the kind common amongst 12 year old boys where both are still too scared

and still too innocent to throw an actual punch. Finally, C.J. spoke up again.

"What's your fucking problem, dude?!?"

"Me?!?" It was all I could manage for a second, and then, "How the hell did you run all the way up here so fast?"

"I didn't run anywhere, dickhead. When you guys started counting I ran about halfway in and then started sneaking back up here, crawling almost. My plan was to stay behind all of you until you made it to the back, then wait for you to bunch up so I could get as many of you at once as I could. Then all of a sudden Becca starts screaming and you all start running up here, ruining my fuckin' plan. I figured I would jump and least get a couple of you." Then he turned to face Becca. "By the way, why'd you fuckin' cheat and yell? You know you didn't see me."

We all turned to Becca, and her lips began to tremble. Even in the poor light it was easy to see that the color had drained from her face. "Bbbbut I don't understand," she said. "I did see you, way back in the far corner."

We were all confused, but Becca was more than that. She was downright terrified.

"You were right behind me when I took off!" she continued, choking on tears now. "How did you get up here?!?" She stepped up and started slapping at C.J.'s chest, her tears coming full blast now.

"That's bullshit!" C.J. shouted, catching Becca by the wrists. "I was not behind you! You didn't see me! It took me ten minutes to crawl back up here and I've been hiding ever since. Now what the FUCK, Becca?!?" He was trying to sound tough, but it wasn't hard to hear the underlying fear that had crept into his voice, too.

Becca shook her head and her crying had morphed into sobbing. The rest of us were still too confused or shocked to do anything. Finally, Becca stopped moving her arms and managed to choke out some words that actually made sense. "You're really scaring me, C.J. I mean it. Please, tell me how you got up here." She began to sob again and I think that's when we all realized how truly shaken up she was. Including C.J.

He pulled her close as she buried her face in his chest, soaking his Pearl Jam t-shirt with her tears. "Hey Beck?" His voice wasn't filled with the harshness anymore. "Becca, look at me," he said as he gently pushed her away from him. "Becca I really don't know what you're talking about. Now where was it that you thought you saw me?"

"I DID see you!" she snapped, and then, calming slightly, "I told you. In the far back corner, up against the fence. You were crouched behind a big mound of dirt, looking into an open grave."

This last part helped all of us make the transition from confusion to fear. An open grave in a cemetery is naturally a creepy thing. An open grave in a cemetery in the middle of the night is something different all together. It was terrifying. At twelve years old one couldn't help but imagine that an open grave was a portal to a place full of Zombies and demons, or worse yet, a place where those evil things could come back into our world.

We all stared at Becca, silent. Finally, she was the one that broke the silence.

"You don't believe me? Fine. Come with me and I'll show you the grave."

Looking back, I'm sure we all wanted to stop her, but Becca was already thirty feet ahead of us, marching off into the dark void of the cemetery again before any of us could say anything to her. So having failed to stop her, we moved on to option two, which was to follow her.

Becca's march transformed into a frantic dash and it really is a miracle that none of us broke one or both ankles chasing after her that night. As we all neared that remote corner of the graveyard I can remember being worried that if there was an open grave back there we'd better slow down--I really didn't want to fall into the damn thing. As it turned out, there wasn't anything to worry about.

Becca stopped in front of us as abruptly as she'd started, just shy of the wrought iron fence that enclosed Antioch Cemetery. The rest of us caught up a moment later and surrounded her so we could look down at…

Nothing. There was no grave. There was no pile of earth for anybody to hide behind.

I instantly wanted to get pissed off at Becca for jerking us around, and I probably wasn't the only one, but when I turned back to see the tears streaming down her face again, any ill feeling I'd had towards her was instantly gone. There was no questioning that Becca really did believe she'd seen C.J. back there, staring into an open grave. She fell to her knees and continued to sob, and that's

when the rest of us finally moved in to comfort her.
"Hey," C.J. said, kneeling beside her. "It's no big deal. It's dark as shit in here. I can see why you probably thought you saw something in all these shadows."
Becca shook her head but didn't look up. "I didn't see something, C.J. I saw you." What she said next scared me more than anything else. "You were crying."
Big Clint spoke up this time, unable to hide the pre-pubescent twang in his voice. "What do you mean--he was crying, Beck?" Only "mean" and "crying" came out as "mane" and "crine."
Becca looked up at him, and then turned her head around at all of us, before staring right back at C.J. "I don't know, at first I just reacted and shouted out. I turned to run and that's when I realized you were crying. I almost stopped to come back to you but I could hear you--I could feel you chasing me so at that point I figured maybe you weren't crying after all, and that I was just seeing things." She gave a pitiful little laugh then as the tears came again. "I guess I was."
There was no logical explanation as to why Becca had seen what she'd seen, other than the shadows really were playing tricks on her. Seeing her that upset and confused was one of the scariest things I can recall from my youth (up to that point anyway).
We helped Becca up and decided that we'd all had enough "Ghost in the Graveyard" for one evening. We walked back to Becca's house in near silence--the only sounds were Becca's occasional sniffles. When we got back inside we attempted to salvage what we could of the evening, but after an hour it was clear that Becca (and probably the rest of us too) were still pretty shook up. We decided to wake up Becca's Mom and Dad and told them that Becca wasn't feeling too good--probably too much cake. We weren't about to tell them the truth.
The decision was made to call all of our parents to come pick us up (I got grounded because I had told my Mom that I was sleeping over at Clint's farm). C.J. was the only one that didn't call his folks because they were too drunk to drive and they would have just beat his ass for the trouble any way. He was the first of us to leave. He hopped on his Huffy and started pedaling back towards town. At the end of the driveway he turned back and gave the rest of us the finger and a smile--a last ditch effort to make light of the evening.
It was the last time any of us would see him alive.

Oddly enough, every one of us went on a separate, "end of summer" vacation that following week. Everyone except for C.J. He spent the next two weeks riding his Huffy down to the tennis courts at the town park so he could smoke camels with High School hard-asses.

And he went swimming.

There were many places around Conscience to swim in the summertime. The pool and spa store, the golf course ponds or Kell's creek. Rarely was it ever done in someone's actual pool. The preferred spot for those adventurous souls was known as Cobb's Iron Bridge. It was a ninety foot long monstrosity that towered four stories above the Cahokia River, built to support the heavy coal trains of the area. On the morning of his death, C.J. would have ridden his bike a mile and a half down the tracks to get to the bridge. Once there, the idea was to creep out to the middle of the bridge and wait for a train to come, then jump off at the last minute before you went head to head with 8,000 tons of steel. Most of us that had actually jumped would tell you the trains missed us by mere inches, but in reality they rarely got within twenty yards of us before we chickened out and leapt into the deep water below.

Nobody knows for sure if C.J. was dodging trains the day he died, or just jumping for fun. He was a strong swimmer and the water was plenty deep enough so I doubt he'd hit his head. There were no witnesses as to what happened. He had gone to the bridge by himself, just a poor kid whose family couldn't afford the money or effort to go an actual vacation. Anyway, as I mentioned earlier, his body was found three miles downriver from Cobb's Iron Bridge. The coroner said he'd been in the water for four days before he was found. After the first day he didn't come home, his folks probably assumed he was staying over with a friend because he did that a lot in the summer. They never realized it was because he was tired of their drunken shouting matches. After the second day his folks sobered up enough to get worried and notified the Sherriff, who began a search of the town. On day three two deputies found his bike parked on the West side of Cobb's Iron Bridge, and early on day four they found him face down on a sandbar, the early stages of decomposition already taking root, and minus 4 fingers as a result of a family of snapping turtles finding him before the deputies.

I remember my Dad telling me the news that night. I should have known something was up. Dad never talked to me alone like that unless I was in serious trouble. After that summer, his solitary visits would also come to mean that someone had died.

I remember being sad and a little confused, because up until that point I'd never had a friend die so I wasn't sure how sad I was actually supposed to be. I decided I wasn't going to cry at the funeral.

I remember the visitation was nice. They played a lot of Pearl Jam. They were C.J.'s favorite.

I remember it was still hot outside but the funeral parlor was freezing inside. I expected to become overwhelmed with emotions when I saw C.J.'s lifeless body in the coffin but I did O.K. The funeral directors had done a good job of hiding the effects of the four days he'd spent water logged in the river.

I remember that he looked peaceful. And I remember thinking, even then, that this was a cliché observation, but true nonetheless.

I remember that his parents had him dressed in his baseball jersey. It was one of the few things they ever did right for him.

I remember staying at the funeral home for a long time before C.J. was finally loaded into the hearse and we all drove out to a place that we were quite familiar with.

Antioch Cemetery.

The funeral patrons all filed in, but Clint, Amy, Edie, the Twins (Wendy and Wes) and I waited at the gate so we could walk in together, just as we had two weeks earlier.

Becca hadn't gone to the visitation, but when we looked back she was standing across the street in her front yard. I waved and she waved back, but she didn't move.

The rest of our gang, minus Becca, started following the crowd to the grave site. We marched past the flag pole which had served as "home base," past the crypt where C.J. had hidden, and past the big oak that marked the halfway point. We walked on, all of us looking down at our feet, thinking of the four or five previous summers we'd spent together with C.J. When I finally sensed that I had reached my father's side I looked up. My breath caught in my throat and my heart froze at what I saw.

C.J.'s parents had managed to do one more decent thing for him. They'd picked his grave location in the far back corner of the cemetery, right up against the fence. It was a spot we'd all seen before, and in the sunlight it was beautiful. There was a large mound of dirt covered by obnoxious, carpet-like fake grass next to C.J.'s coffin. I guess that's supposed to make it easier for the families. When I thought about all that dirt being thrown on top of my friend I finally broke down and cried. I was relieved to see that my friends were all crying too, and at some point during the graveside service Becca had walked over from her house, and she stopped next to me.

She was the only one that didn't cry that day, because she'd already shed her tears two weeks earlier. She stood there, smiling, because she knew better than any of us that C.J. was at peace. After all, he'd hand-picked his final resting place.

We should all be so lucky.

The End.

Case #16773

Anthony Hanks

Anthony "Tyson" Hanks is a fan of horror—both literature and film. He wrote quite a bit when he was younger but was struck with a tragic case of adulthood. He has recently taken up the hobby again and is thrilled that some folks have deemed his work worthy enough to show the public. He has yet to receive a literary award, but he did get a gold star on a middle school English paper once. He lives in Florida with his beautiful wife, and when he isn't writing fiction, fishing or working the dreaded "day job" he--along with a couple of fellow horror nerds--writes film, book and haunted attraction reviews and articles for their horror blog www.nerdcronomicon.com .

CLAYTON HILL SANITARIUM

CLAYTON HILL SANITARIUM

Dark Verse

Physician: Dr. Salam
7128-DV758JJ

Kristen Lester
Drew Downing
Anthony Crowley

The Blackened Witch by Anthony Crowley

I came upon this spiritual land for a chance to awaken new beginnings,
My face and eyes are frosted pale ,since my innocent heart stopped forever beating,
I am a shadow of my former self, enriched with words of divination and folklore,
I believe in a higher destiny,
A clearer path of thoughts and traditions of sorcery,
The 'Book of Shadows' lay upon my illuminated and mystified altar,
I draw down the wicked moon with wand in my hand,
I am the forbidden priestess,
Shall make my apocalyptic approach and I initiate thee I stand…
'Pentacle of Love, Shine so bright'
Pentacle of fire, give me eternal light'
I invoke the damned, and I will evoke with no curse on me or shame,
Magus of fire, reaches out to me within,
Phallus of evil and desire, shields around like a serpents blessed penetrated skin,
I open up like a crimson flower from another wiccan world,
My tempting chalice fills with goodness that I demand,
The ritual has made me feel spiritually protected and attained,
The general enters my circle and takes me in chrome weighted chains,
I feel strong, yet weak, like a ghost in my veins,
As I'm taken to my sentenced holy abode,
A chilling chamber I leave ashamed,
The fire rises higher, but a brightened doorway I can now clearly see,
I sense strong burnt smoke and flaking sparkling ash,
I have deep thoughts in myself, I am feared, but know my name,
I am punished with the leathered whip of a lash,
The general fears in denial to blame,

I slowly drift now from this forsaken soil of Salem,
I will live forever as one, my witchery of darkness shall appear again and again..

Case #14780

Anthony Crowley

I have always been writing since the age of 6, I used writing as a secure world to escape to,as I was growing up through my childhood ,I entered into literary competitions and did rather well.My grandfather was also an influence to me,and himself was also a Poet and knew the meanings of many words. The old classic horror movies was also a big influence to me,I began visualising various forms of horror and fantasy and it encouraged me even further to create my own worlds and visions.

One of my lifelong interests is divination and ever since a child,I always felt comforted about the afterlife,i felt much more secure around this subject and the living ones. I have written articles for withcraft magazines and Cornish history,I also had work previously published in horror monthly's and In the year 2010, The Light of Keeps Passage,was published worldwide,the story did rather well and was also used as a textbook in several educational establishments,such as,Harvard College,USA.

In the future I shall fully extend and revise an updated edition of the supernatural story. In my interest of writing ,I have also written many song lyrics,due to previously at one time being an entertainer for some years and a singer in two rock/metal bands. The present day, My world is always focused and determined into literature and art.

I want to also begin to draw and paint and create extra visions towards my writings.I also began to have more control over my work too,under the name of crowley creations,my official publishing name. When I write either a story or poem,My mind instantly goes into those places where others fear or afraid to witness' Currently I have a forthcoming long awaited supernatural Occult Novella 'The Mirrored Room,which shall hopefully be released late 2013. There shall also be a Spanish language edition of this Novella. The book in question is also nominated for best cover artwork of 2013 at 'AuthorsdB' The Global Authors database.

CLAYTON HILL SANITARIUM

There Is Something at My Window
by Kristen Lester

There is something at my window
Tapping, scratching, beating against the cold, dark glass
There is something watching me through my window
I feel it's cold, dead eyes locked on me as I sit at my desk
Nothing but the weak light of the desk lamp to see with
It taps again and racks it's dirty, gritty nails on the dark glass
I see it smiling its twisted smile, and see its gnarled, jagged teeth
There is something coming through my window
The cold air from outside rushes in and the thing crawls over the window sill.
There is something standing in my room now
Skinny with long pale limbs that dangle to the floor.
The lamp light makes the yellow stains on its horrid teeth pop out
There is something coming towards me in my room
Slowly and dragging its long arms on the floor and smiling that sickening smile
No time to move, no time to scream, no time to breath
That something is a few inches from my face now
And its teeth are sinking in.
I jolt out of bed and look to see my room dark, empty, and silent
"Ah just a dream" I thought as I snuggled back in my blankets
But then my heart stopped…for there was something tapping at my window…

Case #44208

Kristen Lester

Details not released at this time.

CLAYTON HILL SANITARIUM

Twas the (Undead) Night Before Christmas

by Drew Downing

'Twas the night before Christmas as I lay with my spouse
while an ominous dread crept through our dark house.
No stockings were hung—as adults we don't care—
though scents of bourbon and nog did hang in the air.

Our cat, "Mama's Baby," was curled in her bed
as visions of mousies danced through her head.
My wife slumbered deeply—in no mood for love—
while I trembled in fear at the sounds from above.

A THUD! A CRASH! A shriek and a clatter.
Moaning and groaning, a shout and a splatter.
Paralyzed by fright, I remained on my back,
watching the ceiling as it creaked and it cracked!

The thump of heavy footsteps now on the roof.
A menacing snarl—AHH!—not a goof!
The scraping of brick, loud grunts, and a scuffle.
Groans, cracking bones—a real kerfuffle!

It must be said here that there is no St. Nick.
So who's on the roof? Answer me quick!
I nudged my sweet beau in an effort to wake her.
She stirred and she huffed but I just couldn't make her!

"Be a man, dammit!" My Dad always said.
I sat up, donned slippers, and tip-toed from bed.
A noise in the front room made my fragile heart race;
the sounds of scuttling from the grand fireplace!

As I crept closer and peered through the gloom,
I saw tiny creatures plod through the room.
Clad in tights, felt hats, and pointy felt shoes,
they appeared to be elves, but was this a ruse?

I drew a deep breath, then flicked on a light.
The creatures turned toward me and OH! What a sight!
They were elves to be sure, but like none I'd seen.
Their mouths dripping blood; eyes—cold, blank, and mean!

They moaned and they groaned and all staggered toward me.
I gasped and marveled at this nightmare before me!
Retreating apace, to the dining room I led,
this diminutive hoard—The Elfin Undead!

I glanced at the table and cursed once in vain,
for all that lay there was a large candy cane.
The elves nigh upon me, I grabbed it in haste,
snapped it in two then began to lay waste.

With a shard in each hand, I stabbed and I slashed
at their tiny elf heads—their brains I did gash!
At the ruckus my wife opened the bedroom door
and screamed bloody murder at the hideous gore.

"No time to panic, dear!" I shouted in reply
as my candy cane dagger pierced a tiny elf eye.
"Honey, behind you!" she yelled and I saw
elves swarming from the kitchen; we both stared in awe.

Back in the bedroom, I shut the door with a SLAM!
Raised the blinds at the window, jumped back and said,
"DAMN!"
Zombie elves filled the yard; their moans were emphatic.
I lowered the blinds and exclaimed, "To the attic!"

Mama scooped up her Baby, who cowered on the floor.
We hurried up the steps as they broke down the door.
As I raised the ladder and pumped a bloody fist,
an elf glared up at me and emitted a hiss.

Only then did I notice the chilly night air,
tickling my face and toussling my hair.
I looked at the wall but saw clouds, sky, and snow.

The moonlight shone through with its soft pale glow.

From behind me I heard a most ghastly wail,
I turned to see my wife ghostly and pale.
I saw the mangled sleigh and the eight dead reindeer—
blood, bones, and entrails! My eyes filled with tears.

Then, stomach-churning sounds—gnawing, chewing, burping.
In a darkened corner, a vile evil was lurking.
Detecting our presence, it rose to its feet—
a great bulging beast stuffed full of 'deer meat.

Spattered in blood from his head to his toes,
howling and growling and snorting his nose.
With a bearded sneer and a belly swollen and thick,
dear me, it must be! The Zombie St. Nick!

He lumbered toward us to continue his feast.
We took a step back from the ravenous beast.
My foot brushed an object lying on the floor—
a multi-pronged antler; my heart, how it soared!

I snatched it up firmly in my trembling fist,
and eyed Undead Santa; now I was pissed!
Those poor slaughtered reindeer—such a cruel fate!
I charged the fat man in a fury of hate.

With the antler I stabbed at his bulging old belly.
It exploded and drenched me in bloody red jelly.
I slashed at his throat and he let out a wheeze,
swayed for a moment then dropped to his knees.

I paused to look him in his lifeless grey eyes—
the man I once cherished but now so despised.
With my heart now empty of holiday cheer,
I exacted vengeance for those poor dead reindeer.

"This one's for Dasher! This one's for Vixen!
One for Comet, one for Cupid, Donner, and Blitzen!

Oh yes! One for Dancer, you vicious vile cretin!
And one more for Prancer to end this ass-beatin'!"

The antler I dislodged from his face one last time
and he fell to the floor, having paid for his crime.
I turned to my wife who was now ashen-faced.
I said, "Santa's dead," and then we embraced.

As we gathered our wits and steeled ourselves
to rid our fair home of zombified elves,
I exclaimed with grim cheer in the stark lunar light,
"Wary Christmas to all, on this, Undead Night!"

Case #72064

Drew Downing

Drew Downing lives in Silicon Valley with his wife and a cat. His short fiction has appeared in Stymie and The Molotov Cocktail, as well as in two anthologies—First Person Imperfect and Further Persons Imperfect. He writes mostly to clog his laptop's hard drive with long-neglected drafts of unfinished stories. He'll spare you his likes, dislikes, hobbies, and other personal flotsam since—let's be honest—you probably don't care. Now if you'll excuse him, he must get back to finding things to do other than writing a novel.

CLAYTON HILL SANITARIUM

On the
Record

A Moment With Patrick McCabe

Words by Andy Squires.

Patrick McCabe is an award winning Irish novelist and playwright. Two of his novels, The Butcher Boy and Breakfast on Pluto were shortlisted for the Booker Prize and also turned into critically acclaimed films directed by Neil Jordan. His latest book Hello and Goodbye is actually an amalgamation of two shorter novellas, Hello Mr Bones and Goodbye Mr Rat. He talks to Sanatarium about his influences, the challenges of writing for stage and screen, and his thoughts on the future of publishing.

Q. Thanks very much for taking the time to speak to us.

Sure.

Q. The new book, Hello and Goodbye, comprises of two stories published as one novel. Was that always the idea, was it a definite decision to publish the two together or was it something that came about while writing it?

Well it kind of grew into a double thing, they had similarities but I didn't set out to do that. It kind of became apparent that it would work and then it took the shape of the old fashioned 70's double features, the hammer double bill, where Night of the Demon and Curse of the Demon, or Blue Velvet and Eddie Blue play together, you know the kind of double feature that you used to get in repertory cinemas.

Q. Two stories for the price of one, which is good for the reader as well.

Well I hope so; I mean it should be very reader friendly, a lot of books these days tend to be very long and very wordy and everything. I never seem to meet anyone who reads them that isn't in the publishing world. To be perfectly honest I'm sure they're very good but I don't know that people have the time to read 1000 pages. I may be wrong but I never seem to encounter anyone who's read them. It's a real investment; you know I think something like 'Breaking Bad' delivers that now in the way that novels used to. I've just finished watching it and it's such a big meal of a thing, it's what people used to do with the novel.

Q. Looking back, you had a lot of success with The Butcher Boy and Breakfast on Pluto. I read a quote from you while you were writing The Butcher Boy where you said you weren't really bothered if it ever got published, it was all about telling the story. Is that still the way you feel?

Yeah it is, probably more so now than ever because I think that you get into this world of the career novelist, some people get trapped into a sort of one track lane whereby it's set up, do you win prizes, do you not win prizes, do you do this interview, do you not do that interview. Whereas all I was interested in was discovering a style of my own and going wherever that took me, not going where somebody else wanted to take me. And sometimes it took me into the limelight and sometimes it dumped me in the boom box but as long as I was faithful to the style and the voice that I was trying to capture then I was happy. I am actually happy that that's how it has worked out.

Q. In the long run I suppose the only person you are really writing for is yourself?

That's true; it's certainly true for me. The guy who wrote Breaking Bad said he stayed in Virginia for as long as he could because he felt that if he went to LA he would lose his voice you know, and you wouldn't of thought that a movie or series like that would ever have got made, if you think of what it's about. But it did and maybe that came from the conviction he had, and if you don't have that you end up pleasing nobody I think.

Q. Are there any characters that you've created in books up to now, either major or minor, who you'd like to revisit, have you ever thought about giving their own novel?

I have thought about it but it's never really worked out. I kind of have a restless imagination and it'd be going over old ground for the wrong reasons. There is always something new to excite me, life changes and I change and it would be going backwards, that's how it would seem to me. Particularly to something that's been successful, I don't want to touch that, avoid that like the plague.

Q. When you were younger, growing up, who were the writers that influenced you?

Brendan Behan. JP Donleavy who wrote The Ginger Man and is kind of forgotten now, he would have been a big influence on my generation because he was a bit of a punk I suppose, of his time, and so was Behan, they would have been influential. As well as them it would have been the usual, people like Joyce, Ian McEwan and the great gothic writers that turn up in this effort.

Q. People like MR James, Henry James?

The James Brothers, as I like to call them, any of those people like HP Lovecraft, LP Hartley. Probably my favourite novel of all time is The Go-Between by LP Hartley who has written a lot of gothic fiction, although that's not particularly gothic, that's more of a lament for the lost English generation of the First World War, I think that would probably be the greatest masterpiece.

Q. That would be your Desert Island Discs book?

It would be actually yeah.

Q. You're living in Dublin now; do you think that will impact on your writing style?

No I've lived in Dublin many times on and off and have very rarely written about it actually. Except as an outsider, as an oblique kind of commentator, but I very rarely write about it. It doesn't really matter to me where I am, I was many years in London and I didn't write a novel about London either.

Q. Some of the words that have followed you around throughout your career would be dense, dark, and macabre. Would that be a fair assessment of your style, there's a lot of humour in your books as well?

I think humorous would probably be fairer. I mean people do tend to focus on the macabre, it's not for me to say I suppose, but I think there are other terms that would be better.

Q. The Butcher Boy and Breakfast on Pluto were turned into films by Neil Jordan. You wrote the screenplays for those, and have also done other stuff for TV; I believe you've got a play on as well at the moment is that correct?

Yeah I'm very interested in theatre now because I find as I get older that working with directors and actors now is kind of healthier, it gets you out of the closet as it were and it's more social. It's too solitary, writing I think, and I don't really like that. For 20 years I wasn't really seeing anyone except maybe to emerge for a public meeting or launch, you just get drunk and go home and it's not really a healthy way to live your life. So I'm very attracted to the stage for that reason.

Q. Do you find the process of writing for stage or screen different to writing a novel?

Yeah they're all different, but ultimately they are about a voice, one that's singular, that is your own and that couldn't be written by anybody else. But you do come at them from different angles really.

Q. I suppose working for stage; there is a lot more visualisation, and thought about what it will look like?

It's almost like you imagine a character going 3D and walking around, you know and it has to stand on its own two feet. You have to engage the audience. A writer I know once said that, in a novel, you can get away with a lot of side-tracking, a lot of rambling and wandering but on the stage, or in a movie, a couple of minutes of dead time is fatal. The audience will get ahead of you, will lose interest in you and you will have blown it. So it's very demanding, both the screen and stage are demanding in terms of storytelling, you've got to be up to the mark.

Q. Is it something you enjoy, obviously you create the characters, create the locations, the world for them to inhabit, do you enjoy passing it over to a director and seeing what directors do with it, what actors do with the work?

Only if I trust the director. If I don't trust them, of course if you don't trust the director then you shouldn't be giving it to them anyway. But sometimes you don't know, some might be un-trusted or unfamiliar with your style or intentions and then it can be disastrous and you'll never want to write another play as long as you live. I have two or three directors that I work with constantly now so I'm pretty secure, but that only comes with time and experience.

Q. And the actors, the interpretation of the roles, have you been happy with most of them?

Not most of them, some of them certainly, and the recent ones definitely. But sometimes actors can get it wrong, sometimes they get it right, like any author can get it right, but sometimes it's too far gone to be able to do anything about it. But by and large I've been well served I think.

Q. In recent years we've seen the emergence of self-publishing and the e-book. What do you think about these in terms of the literary world? Do you think they're a good thing?

Well I think whether they're good or bad I think they are inevitable. No more than the emergence of moving pictures, or the saxophone or anything. We're stuck with it and we just have to see where it lands. I kind of check my own behaviour because I'm not a technophobe by any means, anything that's new I embrace it, but I notice in my own reading habits I don't really use the e-book. I use it for poetry and I use it for comics and research, the kindle, but I don't use it for fiction.

Q. This is probably a question you get asked a lot but what advice would you give to a young or an up and coming writer? Any particular tips you'd give them?

I would tell them to be very wary of trying to make a life out of writing fiction for a living; I would advise to get a few other things in your life sorted before you commit to that because it's a very neurotic way to make a living. It's getting more and more difficult. In our time, if you can say it that way, nobody really expected to make money out of it, expectations were lower. I think it's a generation now that's been reared on relative comfort and they might find it very hard to sustain a life as a writer. I mean it's very competitive now, screen and so on and demand for attention. I think writing, just writing a novel now, is as difficult as it ever was but to capture an audience is getting increasingly more difficult.

Q. With self-publishing, it's a good thing in some ways as it allows people to put stuff out there but that means there's ever more voices vying for attention, trying to find an audience.

Exactly. I'm sure you've covered this in your magazine and I have nothing new to add to those arguments, they are all very valid. Because the democratisation is very interesting but standards are slipping in all sorts of ways, I mean in writing and others but it hasn't been fixed, we don't know what way it is going to land yet, the internet is still being formed. Look at the world of music; it's still in a state of flux.

Q. In a couple of years something else may come along which changes things again?

I think it's very very likely, I mean the pace of change has accelerated such an extent now, you blink and it makes your art almost redundant. It's technology that's changing the world.

Thanks again for taking the time to talk to us.

No problem at all, thanks very much.

Patrick McCabe's new book Hello Mr Bones/Goodbye Mr Rat is available now in shops and online published by Quercus Books.

Where the Horror Happens
With HJ Williams

Can you describe what your workspace is like?

The room I'm sitting in has a split personality – half bedroom, half workplace. As well as writing fiction here, I run my 'day job' business in this space – writing and designing publications about wildlife.

Among the anonymous shelving units and lumps of technology stands this room's only notable feature: an ancient, work-worn desk. It is multifariously scarred – a lot has gone on at this desk. It belonged to my dad, bought second-hand while he was a designer in London in the 1960s (so perhaps 'ancient' is too grand a word, but it's pretty old). He bought it when he made the courageous decision to leave his London job. He set up as a freelancer, working from home and I remember the desk from his studio in the house when I was a kid. When I look at it I can smell the gouache paint and hear his brush in the water jar.

Do you have a go-to gadget / app or service that you cannot live without?

I would have to say my crappy little Fuji compact camera. I use it to photograph the places that inspire me. I always try to keep in mind how important visualisation is in written narrative. Like many authors, when I write I see what I'm describing like a film playing out internally. It's easy to get bogged down in words on a page and forget that what you are trying to conjure is imagery - of place, of person, of expression. In view of this the £30 camera is a pretty indispensible gadget. Oh, and Photoshop of course!

Do you have a set routine while you work?

I recently returned to novel writing after a long break, and I think I'm still re-discovering my routine. A bit like the best stories, the process of writing has not turned out how I expected! I envisaged myself working in the evenings, writing first drafts long-hand (so as not to spend even more time at the computer after 'day job' work). Instead I find myself pummelling away at the keyboard, often in the mornings, a time of day I never thought I'd be able to create anything.

But sometimes I wonder. Maybe all that stuff - routines, environment, technology - doesn't matter as much as we think it does. Maybe if the idea grips you hard enough, you'll write it with a sharp stick in a patch of mud.

What is the best piece of advice you have ever received?

I can't remember where I read it, or who first said it, but it was three simple words: 'Read…write… wait'.

Do you have a final piece of advice for our readers?

Be patient. Don't expect things to come together quickly. Collect ideas over a long period, write them down, mull things over, go for lots of long walks and visit new places. Read a lot. Listen in on people's conversations and look at everyone who passes you in the street. Don't be precious, never be afraid to get rid of anything. Gather about you people that you trust and tell them how things are taking shape and listen to their responses. Don't be downhearted when you get stuck – it won't last. You will find your way past every problem and eventually will know what is to happen from the first word to the last. Then you start to write.

About HJ Williams:

I write paranormal fiction. I suppose the best way to describe my work is 'supernatural mystery': if a crime novel is a 'who-dun-it?', I guess one of my books is a 'what-the-hell's-goin-on?'. My work is eerie, creepy, compelling and full of twists.

I've been telling stories for as long as I can remember and writing has always been an important part of my life. These days factual writing about wildlife pays the bills (well, sometimes). I've recently started self-publishing my fiction output; my debut novel 'Elsham's End' is available on Amazon. I am currently working on a new novel called 'The Shade Clan', which will be available in early 2014.

I live in England, on the Kent coast - a small town called

Folkestone, which has a thriving creative community that I value a great deal. Kent is known as the Garden of England and I gain tremendous inspiration from its varied landscapes, but often from the less garden-like parts!

To find out more about my writing, go to my blog at:

http://hjwilliamswriter.wordpress.com/

We hope you enjoyed the latest issue of
Sanitarium (Horror and Dark Fiction) magazine.

Remember the next issue is realese on the 20th of the month and there will be the usual horror fiction, reviews, news and interviews to sink your teeth into.

If you have any feedback or would like to leave a review please head over to Amazon and share your thoughts about Sanitarium.

Thank you for your time and we salute your
love for all things horror.

Looking for more horror to keep you entertained? Why not check our back issues, they are just waiting for you to download them on Amazon.

Issue 15: http://amzn.com/B00GTYNUXU
Issue 14: http://amzn.com/B00G1P1HNC
Issue 13: http://amzn.com/B00FIOUO1S
Issue 12: http://amzn.com/B00ENO7DK4
Issue 11: http://amzn.com/B00E0Q386S

5399591R00068

Printed in Great Britain
by Amazon.co.uk, Ltd.,
Marston Gate.